HOME BUT NOT ALONE

HOME BUT NOT ALONE

A guide to surviving hassles at home

David Lawrence

Illustrated by Taffy Davies

Marshall Pickering
An Imprint of HarperCollins*Publishers*

Marshall Pickering is an Imprint of
HarperCollins*Religious*
Part of HarperCollins*Publishers*
77–85 Fulham Palace Road, London W6 8JB

First published in Great Britain
in 1994 by Marshall Pickering

1 3 5 7 9 8 6 4 2

A catalogue record for this book is
available from the British Library

ISBN 0 551 02890-4

Printed in Great Britain by
HarperCollinsManufacturing Glasgow

Illustrations by Taffy Davies

Contents

Introduction

Whoever came up with the phrase 'Home Sweet Home' has never been in our house when Dad has overslept, I'm late for school, my mum has one of her 'heads', the dog's been sick, the washing machine has leaked all over the floor, my baby brother has got his head stuck between the bars of his cot, there are only odd socks in my drawer and there's not a clean pair of underpants in the house. At times like this (ie most mornings), home is *not* sweet.

However, this is the real world that most of us live in and this is the world that this book is all about. The world of *home*, with all its mix of good times and bad, of arguments and agreements, and of niceness and nastiness. *Home*, where sometimes you're so happy and sometimes you're just begging to escape. *Home*, where no matter how many people are around, you can feel so *alone*, unsure of what to do or how to respond to what's going on around you.

Home and Alone – until now, that is. This book, whilst not the answer to *all* your difficulties (it contains no clean underwear and no odd socks) will help you get a grip of life at home and start turning some of its sourer moments a bit more sweet. With this book you are *home* but not *alone*.

A quick look at the contents page will show you that each chapter is about a different topic. You do not have to read each chapter in order but you can jump straight in to the one that looks most relevant to your family. (Since every family is very different not all of the chapters may be relevant. For example, if you don't have any brothers or sisters, skip the chapter that tells you how to deal with them!)

Finally, don't expect a quick skim through this book to sort out all your problems at home. The book may help you decide where to start but in the end *you* will have to work at the problems – probably over a period of time.

Happy reading! Happy Home!

Vinny and the Duke of Wellington

When you need to understand
what a family is

INCREDIBLE. UNHEARD OF! The whole family gathered together in one place at one time. Great-uncles, stepsisters and fairy godmothers – the whole lot were here to celebrate my 14th birthday. We would never have fitted into our house so Mum had booked the skittles hall in the local community centre. As I looked around the assembled relatives I realized just what a wide cross-section of humanity was represented in our family.

For starters there was Mum, ridiculously over-dressed, her size 16 figure clasped firmly but awkwardly by a size 12, bright orange evening dress. It tapered to the ankles so much that each step she took only carried her forward about ten centimetres (the short walk from the car to the hall had consequently taken her 35 minutes). Her ginger hair was tied into bunches with green ribbons and she wore long dangling earrings in a shade of green which nearly matched the ribbons in her hair; nearly but not quite. The total effect of her outfit gave her the appearance of an overgrown carrot which was just beginning to learn to walk. Not what she intended, I'm sure.

At the moment she was having a conversation with Granddad who had arrived dressed as the Duke of Wellington, apparently under the misapprehension that this was a fancy-dress 'do'.

'Never mind, Dad,' I heard Mum say, 'it suits you very well. Very becoming.'

'Always wanted to be in the army myself, of

course,' Granddad replied. 'Volunteered for the Guards during the last war, you know, but they wouldn't have me. Too short, they said. Too short, I ask you!'

Granddad had often reminisced about the war and had often reflected on his rejection by the Grenadier Guards – a rebuff which still hurt him so deeply that every retelling of the story was as full of passion as the time when it was first told in the mid-1940s.

'So I said to that toffee-nosed recruiting officer, "What do you mean too short? Too short for what?" Quick as a flash he said, "Too short for the Grenadier Guards, my good man," stuck-up, la-di-da twit. Well, I wasn't having any of that from a bloke like him so . . .'

'You hit him,' interrupted Mum. Granddad could talk for a whole evening about his military experiences and he'd never been further than that Army recruiting office in William Street. He could make that story about being turned down last for hours – goodness knows how long he'd have rambled on if he'd been accepted and actually fought in the war!

Seated across the table from Granddad and trying not to get drawn into the conversation about his war-time experiences was my cousin Vinny. He was 16 years old and profoundly in love with my stepsister Julie who, although aware of Vinny's affections, was totally unmoved by them. Vinny had tracked down Julie at her seat next to Granddad and had attached himself to her. In the past his attempt at friendship with Julie had been seriously rejected by an uninterested Julie but, never one to give up, Vinny had invested in a book called *How to Impress Someone You Really Fancy* which he had found in a second-hand bookshop. The tone of the book was set by the blurb which was printed on its back cover. It read:

In love? Want to impress? Then this book is for you. Award-winning Polish author Dr I. Luvzyu explains how to dress to impress, how to smell to compel, how to act to attract and how to natter to flatter the girl of your dreams. If you follow the straightforward advice contained in this one slim volume, you need never again know the embarrassment of rejection by that special someone in your life. Here are some comments from readers of previous editions of *How to Impress Someone You Really Fancy*.

'I'd never had a girlfriend but after reading Dr I. Luvzyu's book I have had fourteen serious relationships and five offers of marriage.' (Martyn – age 18)

'I used to think there was something wrong with me but since reading *How to Impress*

Someone You Really Fancy I've managed, to speak to lots of girls – one of whom actually spoke back!' (Donny – age 16)

Look our for Dr Luvzyu's next blockbusting, award-winning encyclopedia of human relationships, *How to Distress Someone You Really Hate* – coming soon to a bookshop near you.

Having read the blurb you might think that Vinny would have been alerted to the book's potential shortcomings, but no. He'd got stuck right in and had faithfully acted on its every recommendation. So here he was at my party dressed in a tacky imitation-leather jacket, smelling like a perfume factory and staring intently into Julie's eyes as he quoted a poem ('guaranteed to melt the hardest heart') from Dr Luvzyu's book.

Light of my morning, joy of my heart
From by my side may you never depart.
I have admired you for many a week
And your affection decided to seek.

Mere words can't express just how I care
As I gaze on your face and complexion so fair.
A person like you in life comes just once
So I wondered if you'd like to meet me for lunch.

O please do not spurn me or answer me nay
Or else I'll go mad and they'll put me away.
Life without you is like a bike with no wheels
Going nowhere fast – to your heart I appeals.

To be fair to Vinny he did put his heart and soul into it and to be fair to Julie she did try – for a short while at least – not to laugh out loud. But the internal pressure of suppressed humour was eventually too much to contain and she erupted into floods of giggles. As she paused for breath she managed to splutter, 'Vinny, what are you on about? Where did you get all that junk? Last year's Valentine's cards? You must want your head examined. What was it again? "Life without you is like a bike with no wheels"?' She collapsed with near-terminal mirth once again, before managing to ask, 'Would you do me a favour, Vinny?'

Vinny's face lit up. 'Anything, Julie. What?'

'Get lost,' came the brutal reply, once again uttered through gales of laughter.

Things started to move fast from this point on. Vinny had brought it on himself really but the pain of rejection was so great that, instead of getting lost as requested, he picked up the glass containing the remains of his alcohol-free lager and, without hesitation, emptied its contents over Julie's head. This had a dramatic effect on Julie and seemed to be a very effective cure for her previously uncontrollable hilarity. She screamed and sprang to her feet protesting loudly.

Granddad, who'd had a bit too much rum by this point in proceedings – and who had a bit of a soft spot for Julie – immediately sprang to his feet showing surprising agility for a man of his age. The other thing that he showed was the sharp end of the ceremonial sword which he'd hired with his Duke of Wellington outfit. Waving the blade menacingly in Vinny's terrified face he challenged, 'Insult a lady, eh? Young hooligan. Well, we'll see just how much of a man you are. Draw your sword, sir, draw your sword.'

Meanwhile, Mum, who'd spotted the incident developing from the high bar stool which she'd somehow managed to clamber on to, attempted to hasten to Vinny's aid but misjudged the degree to which her dress rendered her incapable of rapid movement and fell face first from the stool to the floor.

Later, the video which Uncle Roland was shooting all the while made compulsive viewing. Granddad was the star of the show, chasing a white-faced Vinny around the room, forcing people of all ages to quite literally dive for cover as his increasingly wild sword slashes endangered anyone within a two-metre radius of his sword arm. In the middle of this pandemonium, Mum was left rolling around the room. Cocooned in her orange full-length strait-jacket, her cries of 'Get me up, will somebody please GET ME UP?' competing in volume with a lager-dripping Julie's screams of 'Vinny, I'll kill you if Granddad doesn't.' It was very colourful.

Of course the whole thing was a disaster. It was certainly a 14th birthday to remember but not one that I'll remember with any affection. I knew it was a mistake getting our family together – I mean, some of them hardly know each other, not really family at all; or are they? What makes a 'family' anyway? Just people who live in the same house or people who are related or what?

– –

Dear David
As a result of a my recent birthday party where so-called family members caused a riot and spoiled the whole thing, I've been doing some serious thinking about what a family actually is.

Is it just Mum and Dad and kids? For a long time I didn't have a dad at home because my proper dad left when I was 5 – were we a real family then? Now Mum's got married again and I've got a stepdad and a new stepsister called Julie. Are they my family or just people that happen to live in the same house? Do I have to treat Julie as though she was my real sister or are the rules different if your sister's arrived in a package deal with your new stepdad?

The more I think about it all, the more confusing it becomes. I've asked some of my friends at school and church what they think but the trouble is they

*all think different things! So, over to you, Dave.
Sort out my head please.*

Yours sincerely

Steve

— • —

Dear Steve

Well, you've certainly raised a big and tricky
subject. Trying to define what we mean when we
use the word 'family' in one short letter is not
going to be easy because there are so many
different sorts of families in the world. You've been
very honest about the different stages that your
family has gone through. Yes, you were a family
when your real dad lived with you. Yes, you were a
family after he'd left you. Yes, you are a family
now that your mum is remarried! And yes your
family also includes all those distant cousins and
embarrassing grandparents! Even in just your situation you can see that we can define four different
groups of people as a 'family'. For a bit of clarifi-
cation though, let's look into the Bible – it's always
the right place to start.

When you look into the Bible, two things strike
you about what it says about family life. Firstly,
God does care about family life and does explain
how it will work best. But secondly, the Bible is
very real about families that fail to live up to God's
expectations. So, let's first look at what God
intended family to be:

9

1. FAMILIES AS GOD INTENDED

a. The Heart of the Matter

Husbands and Wives
When God first placed human beings on the earth he put the first man (Adam) in a very special relationship with the first woman (Eve). Adam and Eve were told not just to be 'good friends' but to become lifelong committed partners, to stick to one another – through good times and bad – as though they were glued together. In fact, God said that their marriage together made them so close that he saw them as one single person, acting together in love for each other. Ever since then, right at the heart of God's intention for family has always been a husband and wife united to one another in love.

Throughout the Bible it is clear that this relationship between husband and wife is to be specially prized and specially protected. Here are just a few Bible verses on the theme:

A capable wife . . . is worth far more than jewels. (Proverbs 31:6)

(Husbands) . . . be faithful to your own wife and give your love to her alone. Be happy with your wife and find your joy with the girl you married. (Proverbs 5:15,18)

Every husband must love his wife as himself,

and every wife must respect her husband. (Ephesians 5:33)

Wives, submit to your husbands, for that is what you should do as Christians. Husbands, love your wives and do not be harsh with them. (Colossians 3:18,19)

So, right at the heart of God's intention for family is a wife and husband living together in love and commitment.

Children

It is God's intention that men and women living together in the way I've described should have children. Right from the time that Adam and Eve were told to 'have many children' (Genesis 1:28) husbands and wives were expected to provide homes where their children could be protected from evil, provided for and where they could be taught to know and love God. Parents are instructed to teach their children about right and wrong and to show them how to grow up into mature adults. Parents and children are to be open-hearted with one another – to really care for one another in a special way.

Jesus himself was born into a family where his dad and mum loved one another and where his parents' instruction helped him to grow up. This is what the Bible says: 'Jesus went back with his

parents to Nazareth where he was obedient to them
. . . He grew both in body and in wisdom, gaining
favour with God and men.' (Luke 2:51,52)

Parents should still give a high priority to their
children, and children are told to pay special attention to what their parents tell them. All sorts of
other people, like friends, teachers, rock stars or TV
personalities will try to influence your life and show
you how to live but the Bible gives that key role to
parents. Who pulls your strings? Here's God
talking to you – yes, you – through the Bible:

> 'Children, it is your Christian duty to obey
> your parents, for this is the right thing to do.'
> (Ephesians 6:1)

Now you can't get much plainer than that!

So right at the heart of 'family' in the Bible is
Mum and Dad and their children. It's a really
important group and no one and nothing should be
allowed to split it up (until the children get old
enough to leave home, of course!).

But family does not end there. Sure, it starts there
but biblical families don't end with Mum, Dad and
their children. The Bible paints a bigger picture of
family than that . . .

b. The Bigger Picture

The family is much wider than just Mum, Dad and children. There are other people who are related; people like grandparents, uncles, aunts and cousins. The Bible is quite clear that our definition of family must include them as people for whom we care.

In biblical times – and still in some parts of the world today – a 'family' that just consisted of Mum, Dad and children would have been very rare. Also living in the family group would have been other relatives such as grandparents or unmarried brothers, sisters – even nephews and nieces, aunts and uncles.

In the New Testament, Paul writes to Timothy and says that the elderly widows in the church should be looked after by their children or their grandchildren and that by doing this they are fulfilling their 'religious duties towards their own family and in this way would repay their parents and grandparents, because that is what pleases God'.

So our biblical family isn't to be a little closed unit of Mum, Dad and their kids but an open plan network of caring relationships which includes all relatives. But family does not end there. Jesus had some really radical things to say about family which widen our ideas even more. Without denying the importance of the dad-mum-children relationship (as we saw that's how he grew up), he said that there is a special family-type relationship which is to be enjoyed by all of his followers.

He was teaching in a house one day and Mary (his mum) and his brothers came to find him. They couldn't get into the house to see him because of the great crowds so they sent in a messenger to tell him that they had arrived. Unexpectedly Jesus asked 'Who is my mother? Who are my brothers?' He looked at the people sitting around him and said, 'Look! Here are my mother and brothers! Whoever does what God wants him to do is my brother, my sister, my mother.' (Mark 3:33–35)

We're not told what Mary thought of that answer but what is clear is that Jesus wasn't saying she wasn't important to him. What he was saying is that God's family is bigger than just Mum, Dad, brothers and sisters; God's family is made up of everyone who loves him enough to obey him. That means that your family not only includes parents, brothers and sisters, grandparents, and all your 'natural' relations but also *every* Christian as your brothers and sisters!

So in your church family you have all sorts of people; young, old, married, single, handicapped, rich, poor, etc. God loves them and has brought them – and you – into his family where the golden rule is 'Love one another', where He is Father and where Jesus is Big Brother. *But family does not even end there!*

c. Families with Open Doors

God's plan for families was that they would not just exist for their own sake, but for the sake of others. Look at what he told Abraham: 'I will give you many descendants and they will become a great nation . . . I will bless you so that you will be a blessing . . . and through you I will bless all the nations.' (Genesis 12:2,3). Families-as-God-intended are supposed to be a blessing to others, to have 'open doors' to people that need help.

Sometimes in Israel travellers would pass through the land and God's families were instructed to care for them and give them food and shelter. Sometimes the travellers decided to stay with the families in Israel and to become their servants. When they did this they were included in the household of the Israelites – sort of adopted as family members.

God wants families today that have open doors to a needy world and who are prepared to take in and help people who need to experience the love and security of a family.

So although in the Bible 'family' starts with a very small number of people relating together in a very special and close way, it also widens out to include other relatives, all Christians and even friends and neighbours in need. This diagram may help explain God's family circles.

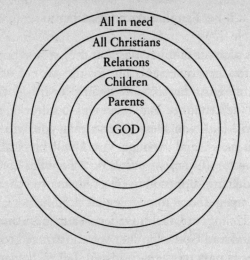

2. FAMILIES THAT FAIL

Wouldn't it be great if family life worked as God intended? But choose almost any family and you'll find a family that in some way has failed to live up to God's ideal. A husband who has failed to love his wife – perhaps even gone off with another woman. A wife who has ignored her husband's feelings. A child who has disobeyed parents (unthinkable!). Relations who don't speak to each other. Churches where people are left isolated and alone.

The examples of failure are seemingly endless and certainly depressing. If you've been in a family that has failed, then you know how hurtful it can be too.

It's at this point that it's comforting to know that the Bible doesn't only tell us what families *should* be like – it's also very honest about families that get it wrong, sometimes horribly wrong!

There are few more dismal families in the Bible than King David's. King David was unfaithful to his wife and had a child by another woman who was herself married to one of King David's soldiers. David's son Amnon attacked his half-sister Tamar. His other son Absalom – Tamar's brother – then murdered Amnon in revenge. Later, Absalom plotted the overthrow of King David, his own father, forcing David to run from Jerusalem to save his life. Happy families – or what?

I don't know what your family is like but in this one Bible family we have a husband cheating on his wife, a child born out of marriage, serious sexual abuse between brother and sister, murder, and hatred between a son and his father! Sadly, David's broken family is a bit more like real life for many people today.

But despite all this pain and mess, the truly staggering thing is this: when God was looking around for a human family into which Jesus would be born, he chose David's! If you've got the stamina to read all the long names in Matthew 1:1–17 you'll find Matthew going to some lengths to prove that Jesus was actually descended from King David! Whatever else this shows us, it makes one point very clearly: *no family has failed so badly that God has given up on it.* There is no family situation that Jesus will not get involved with – he's even willing to get involved in yours, Steve, if you ask!

Whatever the shortcomings of your family, don't give up – keep working at making it better. The reason that God shows us in the Bible what a good family should be is not to make us feel guilty when ours fails but rather to show us what to work at to make ours better.

If Dad has gone and you're left on your own with Mum then thank God for her and get stuck in to making family life as good as possible. If a new Dad's come (complete with stepsister) then thank God for them and welcome them into the family. Respect them and care for them as best you can and pray for help to come to terms with all those churning emotions inside which sometimes spill over into anger and resentment. Try to talk about your feelings, not just bottle them up, and try to spare a thought for how other people are feeling as well – it's hard for them too.

I'll write it again. Whatever the mess that you might feel exists in your family God has not given up on it, so make sure you don't either.

Anyway, Steve, I hope all this helps a bit towards getting a handle on what family should be and what even the most damaged families can aim to be.

Yours helpfully, hopefully

David

A Dog's Life

When it's hard to agree

M Y BRAIN SLOWLY managed to focus as I lifted my head from the pillow. I'm not a morning person and it always takes a while to get life back into gear after the pleasure of a night's sleep. This was a particularly sleepy morning and my mind hesitantly crawled through the data which it needed to feed into my system before I could get up.

'What day is it?' I enquired of my memory bank. This was always the most important question to suss out first since I'd once mistakenly risen and dressed for school at 7.30 am on a Saturday. I'd been halfway down the street before the total absence of any of my schoolfriends alerted me to my error. Fortunately no one had seen me or I would never have lived it down, but it was a close thing – too close, so I now always double check which day it is before getting out of bed.

'Think brain, come on.' I pleaded with my grey matter and eventually I remembered that yesterday had been church, football and a visit from Brad – a Sunday. 'Oh no, today must be Monday.' There could be no doubt. OK, next question, what time is it?

I sent my hand on a mission from under the bed covers and instructed it to grab the small alarm clock standing on the chair beside the bed. It returned having accomplished its task and after some negotiation with my Seeing Department I managed to persuade my right eye to open far enough to look at the digital display. '7.15. Oh, stress,' I groaned, 'time to get up.' But despite my efforts to emerge into a recognizable human life-form my brain failed me at that critical moment, shutting down all my systems and sending me back to sleep. The next thing that its numbed sensors picked up was the sound of Mum at close range and talking fast.

'Gary, for the last time, will you get up, you lazy lummox. It's quarter to eight and time you were on your way. I don't know. What's the point of you having an alarm clock if you never turn it on?' It wasn't really a question, at least not one which demanded an answer, but in my confused and dozy state I attempted one none the less.

'Well, Mum, the trouble is if I do set it I never hear the thing go off – it's just not loud enough. Some days I wake up before it goes off and then I hear it, but if I'm already awake then there's no point in it going off. Of course, what I really need is a louder alarm clock that can wake me up in time to hear this one. Then there would be a point to setting this one, I suppose. But otherwise . . .'

Mum interrupted. 'Gary, you're rambling and making no sense whatever, as usual. Come on, it's time to get up. Your breakfast is on the table and I need your lunch box so that I can pack your sand-wiches. Where is it?' I swung my legs out of bed and came to a sitting position, stretched and yawned loudly before saying, 'I don't know. It's here some-where; probably still in my schoolbag.' Mum made for the corner of the room where I had thrown my bag when I'd returned from school last Friday.

'In your school bag? I wish you'd do what you're told and take it out when you get home from school instead of leaving it in your bag all weekend. It's not hygienic; it should be washed as soon as you get home,' she lectured. By this time she had my schoolbag in her hand and was about to open it. As I watched her fumble with the straps, vague warning bells sounded at the back of my brain. Unfortunately I couldn't interpret their significance until it was too late and Mum was beginning to search my bag for the missing lunch box.

'Gary, what have you got in here?' she asked. 'This bag weighs a ton.'

Suddenly everything came into very sharp focus indeed and I instinctively attempted a diversion. 'Mum, you can't say that any more,' I ventured.

'What, exactly, can't I say?' she responded, hesitantly, at last temporarily thrown off course.

'You can't say that things weigh a ton. It dates you terribly, Mum. Tons don't exist any more. What you should say, if you must use such an expression at all, is that the bag weighs 1016.05 kilograms. Of course, it doesn't sound the same, I do realize that, but . . .'

Mum's icy look froze me into silence. 'Gary, shut it. I know what you're trying to do. The issue here is not how many killer whales there are in a ton . . .'

'Kilograms, Mum, not killer whales,' I corrected and then wished I hadn't since it only stoked the fires of her increasing anger.

She continued to delve deeper into my bag as she snapped, 'I don't care whether it's killer grans, kiss-a-grams or kipper flans, what I do care about is why your schoolbag is full of tins of dog food. Gary, what's going on? It may have escaped your notice but we haven't got a dog – or any pet come to that. Where did this stuff come from? You didn't steal it, did you?'

What a strange question! I dived head first into her rising tide of questions, 'Oh, that's right. Think the worst. 'Course I did. Armed with my bike pump and wearing the balaclava that Gran knitted me for Christmas I daringly held up the corner shop, clearing out their entire stock of Pedigree Chum before making a daring escape on my skateboard which I'd left revving outside. Honestly, Mum!'

This response, which I thought to be quite witty, only succeeded in raising the temperature even more. Mum fired back with, 'Don't you try to get clever with me, you sarcastic so and so. The fact is you've got a dozen tins of dog food and we haven't got a dog.'

'No, that's right,' I shouted back. 'We haven't got a dog. And why not? Because you won't let me have one. I've asked time and again and all I get is "no" or "Maybe when you're older".'

Mum, not to be shouted down, replied, 'Gary,

we've talked about this a thousand times. Despite what you say I know who'd end up looking after it. Dogs need exercise, you know, and it'd be me that would have to walk it, wouldn't it. And it costs a fortune to feed them. Who'd pay for that? Me, again. There's not enough to feed us both, never mind a pack of wolfhounds.'

I tried to calm everything down as I explained, 'I don't want a pack of wolfhounds, just one would do nicely and I know it'd need exercise and I know it'd cost a lot to feed. That is precisely why my schoolbag is full of tins of dog food. I thought that if I could prove to you that I really wanted a dog then you might give in and let me have one. So I decided to buy two tins of dog food a week out of my pocket money to prove to you that I would help look after a dog if you let me have one. I kept them at school in my locker but I was running out of space so I brought them home on Friday to hide them under my bed but I forgot to take them out. There you are, now you know.' I looked at Mum hoping to see some reason for hope in her eyes but all I could see was sheer disbelief.

Her mood was confirmed as she said, 'I don't believe I'm hearing this. You've been buying dog food when we haven't got a dog hoping that I would think that such irresponsible behaviour earned you a puppy? Well, forget it. You cannot have a dog and if all you can do with your pocket money is waste it on pet food for pets that we don't even have then you'll find that being stopped quite soon too.'

It wasn't the best start to a week that I've ever experienced. Breakfast was eaten in moody silence and as I made my sullen way to school I reflected that it was all so unfair. I don't know what to do. Maybe I'll get some advice from someone else.

— —

Dear David

What do you do when you just can't agree with your parents and, however hard you try, you just can't make them see sense? My mum and I have this long-running battle over whether or not I can have a dog. I want one and she says no. I've tried all sorts of things to convince her that I'd help look after it but whatever I try just seems to make matters worse and we end up having a row.

To be honest it's not only the dog (or lack of one) that's the problem. We quite often don't see eye to eye on things; nothing mega, just stuff like how loud to have your stereo on and what time to be home at night. Usual sort of things I suppose but how do you work it all out without screaming at each other? Can you help?

Yours desperately
Gary

— —

Dear Gary

Thanks for your letter. You've raised a good question! I'm not going to try to decide whether or not you should have a dog – that must in the end be a decision for you and your mum – but I will try to give you some guidelines on how to handle hassle so that things get sorted out and not left to go from bad to worse.

Incidentally, all relationships occasionally go wrong and some of these guidelines might also help you when you don't see eye to eye with your friends or your teachers.

1. TAKE A LOOK INSIDE

Often arguments and hassles between people are made a whole load worse by the bad attitudes within the people themselves. If someone is acting selfishly or unkindly then it's bound to make things worse whatever the rights and wrongs of the issue that is being discussed. Are you sure that your attitudes to your mum are in order or is there something to get sorted out first? The Bible gives some sound advice:

'Let us stop turning critical eyes on one another. Let us rather be critical of our own conduct . . .' (Romans 14:13) Are you being critical of your mum *before* you've been honestly critical of your own behaviour and attitudes? Are you treating her with respect as God expects you to? Are you accepting her right to make the final decision in the matter? Are you considering her feelings and trying to look at the issue through her eyes. These are all things that are down to you and if you miss out on your responsibility to have the right attitude to your mum, then you'll be for ever having rows with her. Take a look inside yourself and be ready to change if necessary.

2. DON'T DUCK OUT

Sometimes it can be tempting to have a good old shout at each other and then just leave the thing that you were arguing about without ever really sorting it out. The dust settles and everyone gets on with life until the next time the subject gets mentioned and everyone's feelings get stirred up again.

If things are not sorted out they will not usually get better by themselves. I once had a small rash appear on the back of my hand. I thought it would get better if I just left it but over the next few weeks it spread and then it itched and then when my skin began to blister I decided I ought to go to the doctor! She took a quick look at it, gave me some cream to rub on and within a couple of weeks everything had returned to normal. If only I'd gone to get it looked at sooner I'd have been saved weeks of itching and discomfort.

In just the same way if something is causing an irritation between you and your mum you must get together and really talk it through and not keep having heated arguments which don't really settle the issue but just make matters worse. Take the initiative and when you and she are both calm (*not* when you've just been at each other's throats) ask if you can talk it through. Choose a time when you can both be free and then say exactly what it is you want to talk about.

3. SHARE YOUR OWN FEELINGS

When you talk things through with someone that you disagree with there is often the temptation to make out that everything is *their* fault and to start accusing them of all sorts of things. '*You* never listen', '*You* don't care', '*You're* not interested in what I want' are all the sorts of statements that lead a discussion directly back into a slanging match!

Rather than criticizing the other person try explaining how YOU feel about the issue under discussion. For example, instead of '*You* never listen,' try '*I* find it hard to know how to tell you how I feel'; instead of '*You* don't care about me', try '*I* sometimes feel that you haven't got time for me'; and instead of '*You're* not interested in what I want' you could try, '*I* feel upset sometimes when you seem too busy to take an interest in what I'm doing'.

If you use sentences starting with 'I feel' rather than 'You never' or 'You don't' then the person listening begins to be able to see things from your point of view. On the other hand, if you accuse them of being in the wrong they will probably feel threatened and start defending their point of view – it's a vicious circle which just makes them more sure that they are right and you more sure that they never listen!

4. LISTEN

It has often been pointed out that God gave us two ears and one mouth but most of us still manage to do twice as much talking as listening! The Bible offers us some advice:

> 'Listen before you answer. If you don't, you are being stupid and insulting' (Proverbs 18:13).

Well, you can't get much clearer than that, can you? Sure you've got a point of view too, but if you listen politely and carefully to your mum's then maybe she'll be more inclined to listen carefully to yours.

James 1:19 contains some more excellent advice:

> 'Everyone must be quick to listen, but slow to speak and slow to become angry.'

In all honesty when you have a difference of opinion with someone it's easy to do things back to front. First we get angry, then we start putting our point of view and then – perhaps – we listen. The Bible's way is much better – try it and see.

It's as well to remember though that there is a difference between just 'hearing' what someone is saying – and then ignoring it – and really 'listening' to what they are trying to say and trying to understand the thing from their point of view.

If you haven't understood the point that your mum is trying to make then ask her to put it another way until you really are able to see it her way too. There's an old American Indian saying, 'You should never criticize the way someone walks until you've tried to walk in their moccasins'! Try and really listen to what your mum is saying and see what it means to her if your stereo is making the walls shake or if you don't get home at a reasonable time at night.

5. BE CREATIVE

As you listen to your mum and she listens to you try to think of as many different ways as possible of solving the problem; when you discuss things calmly there are often many more possibilities than you first thought. For example, in your letter you mention the issue of whether or nor you can have a dog. At the moment it seems a simple choice; either 'Yes, you can' or 'No, you can't'. Here are a few more options that could arise if you discussed the issue with your mum.

a. You can't have a dog but you can have a different sort of pet.
b. You can have a dog, but not until certain conditions have been met (for example, your mum's income goes up enough to be able to afford to keep it).
c. You can't have your own dog yet but your mum will place an ad in the local paper to see if there is an elderly person in the neighbourhood who would like you to help exercising their dog. (This would be a good option because you would enjoy the dog, help the old person, keep your mum happy and avoid having to pay any bills at all! It would also give you a chance to prove to your mum that you really would look after your own dog if you had one.)
d. You can have a dog but only a small one which needs little exercise and is cheap to keep.

Anyway, whatever the problem, there is normally usually more than one answer and when you talk things through note down as many as possible on a piece of paper.

6. DECIDE

From your list of possible alternatives you should then try to decide on the best one in the circumstances. It may not be all that you want but being ready to compromise – to accept less than you initially wanted – is an important part of negotiating. If you find that you really like one idea but your mum really likes a different one then keep talking and listening until you can agree.

7. BE PATIENT, STAY COOL

Even then you may not get your own way, not even after trying all the things I've suggested! One of the facts of life is that we don't always get our own way in every situation. (It's probably as well that we don't or we'd become totally selfish people.) This advice is not supposed to be a short cut to getting your own way but rather a route towards making mature decisions. However, compromise isn't easy and when we don't get our own way or when we only get a part of what we want then we can get upset and resentful and those feelings are dangerous with a capital 'D'!

'Hot tempers cause arguments' – so in our anger we need to guard against saying anything that we later regret. Better to say nothing than to say something that makes things worse – 'but patience brings peace' (Proverbs 15:18). OK say you didn't get your way but be patient. If you accept the decision and act in a mature way, if you're patient and live in peace with your mum rather than constantly going to war about it then in the end your mum is far more likely to see your point of view.

Above all else, don't give in to the sulks! Sulking is just a way of saying that you're still cross with someone and that you haven't forgiven them for whatever you feel they've done to you. Unforgiveness is a very serious issue. Let's look in the Bible again for some help:

'Get rid of all bitterness . . . and anger. No more shouting or insults, no more hateful feelings of any sort. Instead be kind and tenderhearted to one another and forgive one another, as God has forgiven you through Christ Jesus.' (Ephesians 4:31,32)

The last few words are the most important. Forgive *as God has forgiven you through Christ Jesus*. God forgave us 'through Christ Jesus' when we didn't deserve it and before we'd even asked to be forgiven. If you feel that your mum has wronged you then the right way to respond is with forgiveness – whether she asks for it or not.

It can't be much clearer, can it? Forgiveness means to carry on with life as though the wrong thing had never been done. Whether you get your dog or not I hope you can do that!

Well, Gary, there's a lot of advice here and I hope and pray that it will help you, not only in your negotiations with your mum but also with hassles that you may experience in other relationships from time to time.

Yours helpfully, hopefully

David

Elephants in the Bedroom

When brothers – or sisters – cause grief

DAD STORMED INTO THE ROOM like a typhoon at the height of its destructive powers. 'What on earth is going on in here?' he bellowed. It was more of a threat than a question but nevertheless it drew the standard reply, 'Nothing, Dad'.

'What do you mean, "Nothing, Dad"? Don't give me that "Nothing Dad" business, just what's going on? From downstairs it sounded like there was a herd of elephants up here,' he retorted, still full of threat. (Personally I found the comparison fascinating. How did Dad know what a herd of elephants would sound like if released into Greg's room? Had it ever happened in his experience? If so, when and where – and what was the effect on the floorboards? Who had managed to round up the elephants and how had they got upstairs in the first place? I was interested to find out more but now did not seem like the time to ask.)

Dad looked around and a brief inspection of the room didn't appear to reveal anything too amiss – certainly no prancing pachyderms (look it up in your dictionary!). There was Greg, ten stone of well-developed 15-year-old brother, sitting on his bed looking out of the window and there was me, glasses perched dangerously near the end of my 13-year-old nose sitting next to him and inspecting the Leeds United posters on his wall. So far it all looked perfectly normal and if it wasn't for the muffled whimpering sounds eerily invading the temporary silence of the room we might have got away with it.

'What's that noise . . . where's it coming from?' asked Dad as he continued to look around the small room inquisitively. It didn't take long before the noises were identified as coming from underneath the mattress on which Greg and I were sat, still all wide-eyed with innocence.

'Whatever . . . Get off the bed, you two,' commanded Dad. We duly obeyed, and as we stood so the mattress seemed to take on a life of its own. It heaved and rocked until first a hand, then an arm, then another arm, a beetroot-coloured face and finally the small frame of Matt, out little brother, appeared struggling valiantly into the daylight.

'I hate you, I hate you, I hate you,' he screamed as he virtually flew across the room and started punching me with all the strength of an eight-year-old Lennox Lewis.

'Matt, stop it. Stop it. STOP . . . IT!' Dad repeated himself as Matt's indignation continued to flow out through his fists. Having stopped, Matt's anger collapsed and he ran, crying, from the room. Dad turned on Greg and me.

'I suppose you think that's funny, do you? Proves you're tough, does it? Putting an eight-year-old under a mattress and sitting on him is the in thing for proving your manhood these days, is it?'

'No Dad,' we muttered in unison, eyes fixed on the floor, minds figuring an escape route. There was none.

'Well, would you mind explaining yourself then?'

he asked. As it happened we did mind, but nevertheless Greg spoke up. After all, he was the oldest and it was his bedroom. 'Dad, he's just such a pain. Matt and me . . .

'Matt and I,' corrected Dad.

'No, Dad, it was definitely Matt and me; you were downstairs,' countered Greg, apparently genuinely puzzled by Dad's attempt to correct his grammar. I thought it was going to prompt a 'don't-you-be-so-darned-cheeky' lecture from Dad but, fortunately for Greg, Dad let it pass.

'We came in here to play a computer game; Tom's borrowed a new one from a friend at school. We loaded it up but when I picked up the joystick it fell to pieces in my hand.' Greg was going slowly, hoping that Dad would see where the root of the trouble really lay.

'What do you mean "fell to pieces"?' queried Dad.

'Someone had taken all the screws out of it. No prizes for guessing who,' prompted Greg.

Matt, who'd got over his fit and had appeared at the door of the bedroom to listen to the rocket that he expected us to be getting from Dad, suddenly disappeared again. But not suddenly enough!

'Matt. Matt, come here,' ordered Dad. Matt came here and was confronted by Dad holding a handful of electronic components and black plastic parts that he had gathered from the top of Greg's desk and which, in a previous existence, had been a computer joystick. 'Do you know anything about this?'

It was a needless question. Matt had a well-known addiction to dismantling anything that was held together with screws. When other boys of his age were requesting Thunderbird models, computer games and footballs as gifts for birthdays and Christmas, Matt was asking for power-tools, hammers and pliers. When other children's school-bags were full of games kit, reading books and lunch-box, Matt's was crammed with wire-cutters, spanners and screwdrivers 'just in case'. Asking whether Matt knew anything about the removal of the screws from the joystick was about as necessary as asking Nigel Mansell if he knows how to drive!

Matt's face answered the question. 'Guilty', it said. Dad followed up with a second question before passing sentence. 'Why, Matt? If I've told you once I've told you fifty times – you're not to take apart things that are still useful. You know that, so why did you take the screws out of the joystick?'

'I wanted to see how it works,' sniffed Matt, his trembling lower lip betraying his inner distress. 'And when I took the screws out I put them in my pocket so that I wouldn't lose them, but then I forgot that they were there and I put my trousers out for washing and when they came back clean the screws weren't there.'

'Oh, brilliant. So not only have you destroyed the

computer joystick but you've also bunged up the washing machine with screws. If the pump jams and I have to call out someone to fix it, the bill comes out of your pocket money, my boy.' Dad had been calming but this latest revelation had refuelled the fires of his rage. 'For goodness' sake, why can't you just leave things alone? Go to your room. I'll sort you out in a minute.'

When Matt had taken his sobbing departure Dad turned to Greg and me again. 'And as for you two, you ought to know better than to pick on someone half your size – whatever he'd done. You could have really hurt him under that mattress. What if he couldn't breathe?'

'Then he'd die,' I thought, still smarting at being hassled by Dad for something that was really Matt's own fault. If he hadn't taken the screws out of the joystick none of this would have happened. I began to argue my defence, 'I'm sorry, Dad, but . . .'

'But nothing,' Dad returned. 'You're both on extra chores for the rest of this week, and while you're doing them you can think about how to behave like civilized human beings.'

It didn't seem fair. As always, Matt causes the problems and we get it in the neck. He'll probably get away with a ticking off and maybe the confiscation of an odd screwdriver or two, while we have to wash up after every tea time this week. Little brothers – who'd have 'em?'

Dear David

I hope you don't mind me writing to you but I've got little brother problems at the moment and I don't know what to do about them (sometimes I have a big brother problem, and get equally stuck).

The problem at the moment is that my little brother, Matt, is always getting me and my older brother, Greg, in trouble. He does something wrong but it's us that gets laid into by Mum or Dad. It all seems so unfair and I get really angry with him, which just makes things even worse (I don't want to but I just can't stop myself).

Anyway, a few words of wisdom about how to cope with brothers would be very welcome so over to you.

Tom

Dear Tom

I get loads of letters like yours from people who are finding brothers, or sisters, hard to cope with. Each situation has its own particular problems, of course, but here are a few bits of advice which I believe would help to improve any relationship between brothers (and sisters).

1. LET THEM BE THEM

All people are different and it's sometimes surprising just how brothers and sisters brought up by the same parents in the same family can be so different from one another. It's quite natural though and trying to fight against it won't help. In fact, if you try to change people by forcing them to become something that they are not, you'll just end up with a load of grief.

The secret is to learn to accept one another's differences. Maybe you like certain things and your brother likes others. Or perhaps he does things certain ways and you prefer them to be done differently. Possibly he's revoltingly lively in the morning but needs to go to bed early whereas you don't wake up until morning break at school but manage to stay awake until well past your official bedtime.

Family life is not supposed to be a competition where each person has to prove that their opinions are always right or their way of doing things is the only way. Personal differences do not mean that one person has to be right and the other always wrong, but simply that each of you is different. You enjoy being you and allow your brothers or sisters to enjoy being themselves too.

2. MAKE ALLOWANCES

Brothers and sisters have to live together during some of the most difficult years of their lives. During the time from birth to teens people change in so many ways. As we grow we change *physically* (our bodies change and develop), *mentally* (we can understand more complicated things) and *emotionally* (our feelings and moods go through lots of changes during these years). We don't choose these changes – or even always want them – but we sometimes find that they've happened and we are now a slightly different person than the one we were last week.

Family life can be made much more pleasant if all the people involved take the time to try to understand the changes that are happening in one another's lives and then make allowances for them. You obviously cannot expect a three-year-old to be as responsible as a 14-year-old – you have to make allowances for her age. It would be daft to expect to explain things to your 15-year-old brother in terms that would satisfy your seven-year-old sister, you have to make allowances for the mental changes that have taken place in him.

Learning to make allowances for the differences of age, strength, understanding and feelings between the members of the family will help you relate together better.

3. BE AN ENCOURAGER

We all know how nice it feels when someone bothers to say a simple 'Thank you' or 'Well done' to us for something that we've done. We also know how unpleasant it feels when people are constantly on at us about the way we look, the things we do, the places we go and the friends we keep.

You probably know the old story of the man who was trying to get his stubborn old mule to move. He shouted at it, kicked it and hit it with a stick but all to no avail. It just sat there. He then had a brainwave and took one of the sticks with which he'd been beating the animal, tied a carrot on a piece of string to one end of it and dangled the carrot in front of the donkey. Immediately the donkey got up and tried to reach for the carrot and as the man continued to hold it just out of reach it kept moving forwards in the very direction that the man's punishment had failed to get it to go. The 'encouragement' of the tasty carrot was far more effective than the bashings and beatings.

I don't suggest that you take either the bashing with a stick or the dangling of a carrot literally. I don't think that either will help your relationship with your brother! But I do believe that relationships that are built on the encouragement of kind words are far more likely to succeed than those built on a constant stream of insults and arguments. Go on, I dare you. Give it a go. Try dishing out a few comments like 'Well done', 'Thanks', 'That was good' or 'I couldn't do it that well'. Keep it up for a few weeks and you may well be amazed at the difference it makes.

4. DO NOT OVERWIND

That instruction was printed on a clock that I once had. It did the clock spring no harm at all to be wound up to a certain tension but once you turned the key past a certain point you were in danger of overstraining the spring and causing serious strain to the mechanism inside.

I sometimes think that people should come with a similar instruction printed across their foreheads. 'Do not overwind – this human being will suffer serious strain resulting in possible breakdown if too much pressure is applied!' We all need to learn how to take a joke and laugh at ourselves and there is no harm done in a bit of gentle mickey-taking from time to time. But it is all too easy for things to go that bit too far and an innocent joke turns into a cruel and hurtful insult.

I am sure you know full well the things that wind you up to the point where you snap, and I'm also pretty sure that you know what to say or do to overwind your brothers to the point where they blow up with anger. There is a very simple rule for getting on with brothers and sisters: *Do not over-*

wind. If you're pushing your brothers to the point where they are growing upset or angry you've gone too far, so stop what you are doing before the situation gets out of hand and someone (possibly including you) gets into trouble.

5. RESPECT OTHER PEOPLE'S PROPERTY

You know what it's like, you take your Walkman on the school trip, you settle into your seat on the coach, stick the headphones on, press play and . . . nothing. You turn it off and turn it on again . . . still nothing. You shake it and fiddle with the headphone socket . . . even more nothing. In desperation you open the battery compartment . . . nothing! *Someone* has had the nerve to whip the batteries out of *your* Walkman without so much as a please or thank you. When you get home investigations begin and the guilty party gets the sharp end of your tongue – or worse.

But then, next week, when you can't find your swimming goggles anywhere and you're late already, you just can't resist the temptation to creep into your little brother's bedroom and 'borrow' his. Trouble is they're not adjusted for your head and the elastic snaps when you're putting them on. When you get home he erupts and . . . you can imagine the rest.

Taking what is not yours without permission is wrong and causes a lot of stress. The Bible gives three simple bits of advice which may help.

a. Be Generous

Jesus' lessons about possessions were pretty radical. He taught his followers to be generous and not to hang on to what they had. Here's some of the things he actually said:

> 'Give to everyone who asks you for something, and when someone takes what is yours, do not ask for it back! If you lend only to those from whom you hope to get it back, why should you receive a blessing? Even sinners do that! . . . No! Lend and expect nothing back.' (Luke 6:30,33,35)

What Jesus was saying is that to be generous is a really desirable thing; to be generous you must not be so much in love with your possessions that you put them before other people. If your brother or sister wants to borrow something don't get in the habit of always saying 'No'. Learn to be generous, even when it isn't deserved, because Jesus says that when we do that we are behaving like God Himself who 'is good to the ungrateful and the wicked' (Luke 6:35).

b. Be Thoughtful

'Do for others just what you want them to do for you.' (Luke 6:31).

That piece of advice given by Jesus is sometimes called the Golden Rule of Relationships. The rule applies to every part of family life – the way we talk to one another, the things we say about one another and the way we treat one another's possessions are all included. If you don't want people taking your stuff without asking, don't take theirs. If you want the things that you lend out returned in one piece then make sure you return the things that you borrow the same way. Being thoughtful about the way that you treat others' possessions sets a good example to other family members and maybe will help them treat you as you want to be treated!

c. Be Forgiving

OK, so all this generosity may be thrown back in your face and a brother or sister may take advantage of your kindness. Your things may not get returned or may get returned broken (with or without an apology!). At times like that it is tempting to make big threats like 'You're never going to borrow *any* of my things *ever* again!'

Statements like that are very understandable but very unhelpful and very unChristian. Forgiveness is a really important part of family relationships.

Forgiveness means giving people a second chance when they don't deserve it. It means lending the tape even when the last one was returned all chewed up. It means lending the bike even though last time it came back with a puncture. Forgiveness means that what happened last time is no longer relevant to what is being asked for this time.

People who bear grudges are miserable people and end up making everyone else miserable too, so be a forgiver and spare everyone the grumps.

6. COMMUNICATE WHEN COOL

When something has happened to upset the smooth running of family life, tempers can get frayed and emotions run high (as I'm sure you know!). Trying to sort things out when everyone is really upset is a waste of time. No one is thinking straight and no one wants to listen to reasons for what happened. Usually in the heat of the moment things are said which aren't really meant and which later have to be taken back.

The Bible says that there is 'a time for silence and a time for talk' (Ecclesiastes 3:7). My gran used to say 'Least said, soonest mended'. Both pieces of advice amount to the same thing really; learn when to speak up and learn when to shut up.

However, it is important that issues and problems in family life don't get left unsorted. When everything has died down and people seem to be in a reasonable mood again, go back to them and try to talk the problem through. If you feel that you get picked on because of your little brother's behaviour, attempting to explain that when your dad's having a go at you is not likely to get you very far. But if you go to him when he's cooled down and say something like, 'Dad, I'm sorry for that hassle earlier but sometimes I feel upset when I seem to get into trouble for what other people have done. Can we talk about it, please?' I'm sure you'll get a better response.

Well, Tom, I really hope that you learn to get along well with both of your brothers and that this advice gives you some clues to what you could start to do to make things work better.

Yours helpfully, hopefully

David

4

Summer of Slavery

When you're expected to help out at home

'THERE IS NO DAY in the year quite like this,' I thought, 'the first day of the summer holidays.'

Waking up with the prospect of six weeks of pleasing yourself stretching ahead of you is truly glad-worthy and as I stretched out in my bed I planned my first week of freedom. Today, nothing. Tuesday, nothing. Wednesday, nothing – no point overdoing it, is there.' That brings me to Thursday. Mmmm, maybe a little something in the afternoon – but only if it's sunny. Friday and Saturday, nothing again in order to recover from the exertions of Thursday's 'little something'. Sunday, church in the morning and then probably nothing – well, it is supposed to be a day of rest! I settled back into bed intent on savouring the moment. There is something very luxurious about snuggling under the duvet while the sun is shining through the window. 'Enjoy,' I muttered to myself.

'Jenny!' Mum's trumpeting call cut through the hazy pleasure of my lie-in with all the subtlety of a Guns 'n' Roses song being played at a Communion service.

'What?' I called back abruptly, more than somewhat miffed at my personal sleeping-space being invaded in this way. 'What do you want?'

'It's half past nine, time to be getting up,' she continued.

'Mum, if I'd wanted the talking clock I would have phoned it. It's the holidays,' I reasoned.

'Don't take that tone with me. I know it's the holidays; that's why I've let you lie in to half past nine. It's because it's the holidays and you've got so much time on your hands that I want to talk to you about helping around the house.'

This was a bit of a bombshell. What a strange idea, me helping around the house whilst on holiday. There was something unhealthy about talk like that. In fact, it may even be illegal to make those sort of improper suggestions to teenagers. I bet the NSPCC would have some guidelines protecting vulnerable young people like me from abusive treatment like that. Perhaps there would be a booklet in the library which I could get to show Mum just how much harm such an indecent proposal could do to a developing personality like mine. Adolescence is a very funny age and it doesn't take much at my time of life to tip people over the edge into anti-social behaviour. Surely Mum knew all this. Surely she could not be serious.

'Jenny, did you hear me? I said I wanted to talk to you about helping me in the house during the holidays,' she repeated. So she was serious!

I got out of bed slowly and made my way to the bathroom. 'Maybe I'm dreaming,' I thought as I looked at myself in the mirror. 'What I need is a shock to wake myself up properly.' I filled the basin right up with cold water, gritted my teeth and plunged my head right in. Even though I knew what was coming the icy water made me cry out in shock

– a silly thing to do when your head is under water – and I straightened up spluttering and coughing. It was painful, but it had worked. I was now fully awake and ready to restart the day without any of these intrusive nightmares about 'helping' invading my dozy brain-space. I dried my hair and face and mopped up the water that had sloshed onto the bathroom floor all with the same towel which I left screwed up on my bed. When I arrived in the kitchen Mum was sorting some clothes.

She looked up as I entered the room and said, 'At last, there you are. Now about these jobs . . .'

So it was true; I hadn't imagined it.

'Mum, I can't believe that you're expecting this of me, your only daughter. Don't you understand the word "holiday". It comes from the two words Holy Day and those were days when you were forbidden to do any work at all.' Maybe the academic argument would work – it was worth a try. But it didn't; Mum was singularly unimpressed with my scholarship and for some bizarre reason remained totally consumed with the notion that a little helping about the house would actually do me good. Well, I can understand how it might do her good, and Dad might even get a few perks out of the arrangement but as for doing *me* good, the idea was laughable.

Finally, bowing to the inevitable, I plucked up the courage to ask, 'Well, what do you mean by "a little help around the house"? I don't mind making my own bed, I suppose, and I could lay the table for dinner once a week or so. Was that the sort of thing that you had in mind?' I asked, feeling that I might as well be generous at the outset.

Mum was smiling as she looked up from the pile of washing she was sorting. I thought that she was pleased with my suggestion but apparently she thought I was joking. 'No, Jenny, that's not what I had in mind. I had in mind washing up, Hoovering, dusting, ironing, and emptying wastepaper bins. In fact, I've written a rota here of the things I'd like you to do. I've only put you down for two jobs a day so you've actually got off quite lightly.'

Two jobs a day! What had I done to deserve this? And what jobs they were! Surely Mum realized that washing up meant getting your hands wet, and me with such delicate skin. Hoovering and dusting was even worse. Sophie had once told me that 85% of house dust was actually dead skin that apparently falls off us in invisible blizzards. I just couldn't bring myself to go around sucking up piles of skin into the vacuum cleaner – it bordered on cannibalism, and me a vegetarian. What is more, all the dust swirling around is bound to bring on an allergic reaction. (I'd never had an allergic reaction to anything before but this sounded like just the sort of thing that would be sure to bring on my first ever.)

And as for emptying wastepaper baskets! Why, there was all manner of horrible things in those.

Rubbish, for instance, and gross decaying items like banana skins and face wipes. Once you've used your Zitt-Cream Face-Wipes and thrown them away you hope never again to see them. The prospect of revisiting them days after their burial in my bedroom bin was too ghastly. I began once again to protest my utter unsuitability for this hyperactive household management role.

However, all my protests were in vain. There is no moving Mum when she's made up her mind about something and the 'Summer Holiday Jobs Rota' became a part of my life. Mondays was hoovering and washing up. Tuesdays was dusting and ironing. Wednesdays was bin-emptying and table-laying (why did I offer that?). And so it went on. By the end of the holidays I was worn to a frazzle and more than ready to exchange Mum's 'Jobs Rota' for the less demanding school timetable. Was it all fair, legal and above board? Do parents really have the authority to inflict such hard labour on their off-spring? I think I'll find out. It's only sixteen weeks to the Christmas holidays!

— —

Dear David
Hi! I need some advice. I've read some of the letters that you've written to other people and they seem to make sense (most of the time) so I thought I'd check out my question with you.

My question is, is it reasonable to be expected to

help around the house? My parents use me like an unpaid slave and I don't think it's all that fair. After all, they chose to get married and have me so it's their job to look after me, isn't it? Things came to a nasty head during the summer when Mum got all organized and issued a rota of jobs that she made me do. I had to do two things every day and really gross things too, like emptying bins and Hoovering up dead people.

I'm sure that you can see my problem. I thought I'd try you before contacting the NSPCC. What I'd really like is a letter back from you that I can show to my Mum to convince her about how unreasonable she is being.

I have every confidence that you will be able to help in this matter.

Yours in exhausted desperation
Jenny

— ◄ —

Dear Jenny

Thanks for your letter. You certainly seem to have got very upset about having to help out at home. I don't want to disappoint you but I'm not sure that you are going to appreciate everything in this reply. Anyway, try to read through to the end and think carefully about what I've written before contacting the NSPCC!

Before I give some detailed advice, let's look at a Bible passage which will help to get us thinking in the right direction. It's from Philippians chapter 2.

Don't do anything from selfish ambition or from a cheap desire to boast, but be humble towards one another, always considering others better than yourselves. And look out for one another's interests, not just for your own. The attitude you should have is the one that Christ Jesus had . . . 'of his own free will he gave up all he had and took the nature of a servant.'

These verses contain some really nitty-gritty advice about how we should act towards one another and these principles are true at home, at school or wherever you find yourself. The key idea is to think of yourself as a *servant* not as a *boss*. Bosses order other people around whereas servants help other people along. Let's take each of the letters of 'servant' in turn and hang a bit of advice on each.

1. 'S' IS FOR SACRIFICE

Servants quite clearly are people who do not spend their whole life doing what *they* want to do. In fact, they spend most of their lives doing things for others. This won't always be easy or pleasant. In the passage that I quoted above, Jesus is given as the perfect example of a servant – but it wasn't easy or 'nice' even for him!

It would have been far easier for him to stay in

heaven with his Father than to become a human being; that cost him his glory. Even as a human being it would have been far easier to arrange a comfortable life with a nice house and loads of slaves, rather than be homeless and constantly on the go meeting other people's needs; that cost him his time. Even as a homeless preacher it would have been nicer to mix with the 'in' crowd rather than spend time with the outcasts; that cost him his reputation. Even as a homeless preacher spending time with outcasts it would have been more comfortable for his life to end in peaceful old age rather than on a cross in the prime of his life; that really cost him everything. Why did he do it? Because, in his own words, he 'did not come (to the earth) to be served, but to serve and to give his life to redeem many people' (Matthew 20:28). His life was all about 'giving' not 'getting' and in living that way he set us an example to follow.

Being a servant costs us, too. Practically it costs us our time and it means that we may not be able to please ourselves all the time. But look on the bright side – doing a few household chores is unlikely to cost us our lives!

2. 'E' IS FOR EXTEND YOURSELF

Instead of seeing the things that your parents expect you to do as a prison sentence you could try to think positively and see them as opportunities to learn new skills. One day in the not-too-distant future you may well be having to look after yourself. All the things that are currently done by your parents will then be down to you. Helping out around the house is a way of introducing you to the realities of life – a kind of in-house training programme!

I once heard of a guy who left home without ever having had to make himself even a cup of tea; Mum and Dad had done absolutely everything for him. On his first day away he brought himself some teabags and, unsure what to do with them, he cut them open and tipped the tea leaves into his brand new teapot before pouring in the boiling water! Needless to say when he poured his cuppa, his teacup was full of tiny tea leaves and he just couldn't understand why it was never like that at home – he was sure that Mum used teabags!

Maybe his is an extreme example but it does illustrate the positive aspect of being expected to help out at home. One day you might be grateful for the opportunities that helping out has given you – honest!

3. 'R' IS FOR REASONABLE

Although I hope you are beginning to see helping out at home is actually a good thing, there clearly has to be some way of deciding how much you do of what sort of jobs.

When you were a baby there were probably very few times when your parents expected you to do the ironing or wash the car! But as you have got older there are an increasing number of tasks expected of you. This is only reasonable and, as we've seen, some of these could actually be to your advantage. Sometimes, though, you may feel that what is being expected of you is just too much and at times like that you will need to explain to your parents how you are feeling.

For example, it would be unreasonable of a parent to expect a young person to be left in charge of the household (especially if there are younger brothers or sisters involved) for hours at a time (commonly held guidelines are that children should not be left home alone under the age of 13 and no one should be left in charge of other children until they are 16).

It would be unreasonable for a parent to expect household chores to come before schoolwork. It would be unreasonable for a parent to expect their children to undertake tasks for which they are not physically big enough (for example, a small child trying to reach up to do the ironing could be very dangerous!). And it would be unreasonable of a parent to ask their child to Hoover up dead bodies! (Are you sure that's what you did?)

If you feel that your parents' demands are unreasonable then you should first tell them and try to negotiate a better, more reasonable deal. If you've tried and you still feel that you are in a position where more is being expected of you than you can reasonably deliver then try to find another adult who you know and whose opinion you respect to check it out with them. If they think there is a problem then they will advise you what to do next but if there isn't – you'll have to be prepared to get stuck in to those jobs at home!

4. 'V' IS FOR VOLUNTEER

So far we've been thinking about 'being made' to do jobs around the home. Here is a truly radical thought for you – how about actually *offering* to do them before being asked!

Did you notice in the Bible passage above that God the Father didn't make Jesus leave heaven, become a baby, and grow up to serve others before dying on the cross. No. The Bible tells us that it was 'of his own free will'. Jesus took the initiative and volunteered to come to this grotty old Earth to live and die for us! What an example!

Think of the stir that must have caused in heaven.

Perhaps there were loads of angels that were aware of the need for a saviour to go to earth and they were all hiding in the corners, hoping that God didn't send them. Of course, if told to go, they'd go but they just didn't fancy all that travel and hassle. Imagine the pleasure and surprise when they heard someone actually volunteering to undertake the mission and imagine the shock as they turned to see that the volunteer was none other than God's only son! Well, all that is in the imagination of course but I'm sure that Jesus' willingness to volunteer brought great pleasure to his father's heart – in fact, the Bible tells us that God the Father says of Jesus, 'This is my own dear son, with whom I am pleased' (Matthew 3:17).

Want to please your parents? Want to be on their good side rather than being the target of constant nags and orders? Try volunteering to help out; it's possible they'll be so pleased (shocked, even!) that it could transform your whole relationship with them. It certainly won't make it any worse, so give it a go and get in first with a 'leave it to me' or an 'I'll do it'. Go on, I dare you!

5. 'A' IS FOR ATTITUDE

Jane was the model daughter. She cleaned, washed up, dog-walked and always made her bed. Over the top? Maybe, but despite all that effort she still hadn't quite mastered the art of being a servant because every time she did a job she just had to let everyone else know about it by constantly moaning about what hard work it was and how she'd rather be doing something else and how 'none of her friends had to do all this work'. When each job was finished she'd hang around the house wearing the sort of face that said 'I've been doing other people's job and I resent it'.

You see, it's quite possible to do all the right things but ruin everything with a bad attitude that leaves you and everyone around you feeling tense and unhappy. The Bible says that we should not give 'with regret or out of a sense of duty; for God loves the one who gives *gladly*' (2 Corinthians 9:7). The verse is actually talking about giving money to support God's work but the principle is true of all giving whether it's giving time to help out or giving a hand about the house. If you've got a negative attitude problem then get to work on it. Pray and admit to God that it's a problem and ask his help in sorting it out; ask for the servant-spirit of Jesus to fill you.

6. 'N' IS FOR NO HIDDEN MOTIVES

Jesus didn't become a servant for what he could get out of it; quite the opposite, in fact. He became a servant knowing that it would mean he lost everything. If we are to follow his example (and that's what being a Christian is all about) then we need to make sure that we are helping out for what other people get out of it, not for what we can.

We shouldn't need to be bribed into helping by promises of rewards for a job well done. We should help out and do every job as though we were doing it for Jesus himself. Just think back over the last few jobs that you've done. Are you sure that your motives were purely to help your parents or were you hoping for some token of their gratitude to come your way?

Of course, there is nothing wrong with being rewarded; we all appreciate a 'thank you' or a bit of extra pocket money. But the message is, don't go looking for it and don't get upset if it's not there.

7. 'T' IS FOR THANKFUL

When you start having to (or better still choosing to) get involved in helping around the home you begin to appreciate just how much hard work your parents have to do just to keep the household going. Ever since you were born they have done everything necessary to get you to this point. They haven't always enjoyed it or found it easy and at times they maybe haven't done it as well as they would have liked to, but nevertheless, you are still alive enough to be reading this and to a large degree that is thanks to a lot of hard work by the people who have brought you up.

Now that you are that much older and being asked to be involved you are realizing just what a bore household chores can be. It's a real drag when someone walks their muddy feet across the floor you've just washed or takes the clothes that you have spent ages ironing and screws them up in their bedroom drawer isn't it? This discovery should make you very grateful to those who have brought you up because they have been serving you for years, often with no thanks or encouragement to keep them going. Sure, they decided to have you in the first place but that doesn't make hard work any less hard, or sacrifice any less costly.

Now that you are becoming a servant yourself you will realize how nice it is when someone bothers to thank you for the work that you have done. Try and return the compliment occasionally. Saying 'Thanks' to your parents for what they do for you won't cost you a penny but it will be one of the most precious things that they receive from you.

So to summarize, Jenny, don't be a slave, be a servant:

Sacrificing what *you* want to help others

Extending yourself to do new things at home

Happily meet the Reasonable expectations of others

Volunteer – don't wait to be told

Watch your Attitude

No hidden motives, just a desire to help

Remember to Thank those who have served you

Well, Jenny, maybe not the sort of letter that you wanted from me, and of course you can ignore it all if you want! But I hope that you see the sense in learning to serve and look out for other people's interests, not just for your own.

Yours helpfully, hopefully

David

5

The First Barbecue of Summer

When it's hard to love your parents

WHEN DOES SUMMER BEGIN? Some people go by the date, some people look out for swifts and swallows and some people wait for the temperature to hit 28 degrees. In our household there is a sign more certain than any of these that the promise of spring has turned into the reality of summer; the announcement of the first family barbecue of the year. When Dad dons his apron and appears in the back garden clutching a bag of charcoal in one hand and a box of firelighters in the other you know that summer has arrived.

Dad is convinced that he is God's gift to outdoor cookery and has consequently nominated himself Master of Ceremonies at all family barbecues. He insists on taking charge of every detail from beginning to end (but strangely 'the end' always stops just short of any washing up that needs doing). Mum, on the other hand, always treats these occasions with a mixture of gratitude at not having to cook and reservation about having to clear up the devastation that inevitably results from Dad's handiwork. One particular occasion comes to mind from last year.

As I returned home from school I was greeted at the gate by Mum who was going out.

'Hello, love. Had a good day?' (She always asks me that but never stops to hear the answer just in case it is 'No'.) She continued, 'Your father's come home early and suggested that we have a barbecue so I'm just popping down the shop to get a few burgers and buns.'

'Yes, and to keep out of Dad's way,' I thought as I carried on into the house. Dad was in the kitchen trying to prise apart two frozen sausages with a carving knife. It was not a sight for the faint-hearted!

· 'Oh, hi, Alex. Bet you didn't expect to see me here. Got away early for once. Thought we'd have a barbecue so I'm just getting everything ready. The secret of a successful barbecue is in the preparation. Preparation and patience, that's what it takes; preparation and patience.' This was Dad's standard pre-barbecue speech, I'd lost track of the amount of times that he'd told us that you needed 'preparation and patience for a good barbecue'.

'I'll get changed and give you a hand if you like,' I volunteered although I knew the answer that I'd get before I even offered. He'd say 'No'. He always did; that's the main reason I volunteered!

'Oh, no need. I can manage – but thanks for offering,' he duly responded, right on cue.

By the time I'd got changed Dad was in the back garden so I sat on the lawn to watch the Master, whose left hand was now swathed in bandages, set to work. As always it was like a well-run military operation. The barbecue itself was placed to take maximum advantage of today's wind direction and Dad was painstakingly piling individual pieces of charcoal on top of a complex pattern of fire-lighters which he'd arranged in the base of the barbecue. After several minutes' work he'd arranged four pyramids of charcoal each sitting on its own fire-lighter.

It was just at that moment that Jamie, my kid brother, returned from school. He threw the back gate open and ran down the path as though he was being chased by a dog. It turned out that there was a very good reason for his behaviour – he *was* being chased by a dog, a very large red setter who belonged to a family that had just moved in down the road. In case you don't know, red setters are famous for their long red hair, their gentleness and for the large streak of lunacy that runs right through them. This one only wanted to play but Jamie, who knew nothing of the mental instability of these creatures, feared the worst and fled straight indoors slamming the door behind him.

The red setter, deprived of his potential play-mate, decided to do a couple of circuits of the garden before returning home and he was on his second lap when, for reasons known only to himself, he tried to hurdle the barbecue. Sadly, his ambition was greater than his athleticism and he rather spectacularly crash-landed in a heap of charcoal and firelighters. Dad, who'd been watching this extraordinary performance of canine vandalism with mouth agape, made for the dog all of a rush and the startled animal regained his senses in time to clear the garden fence before Dad got at him with the barbecue tongs.

'Stupid thing. People that let their dogs run loose like that ought to be put in a dogs' home,' he thundered.

'Don't you mean the dogs ought to be put in a dogs' home?' I asked, thinking that in his anger he'd got his words mixed up.

'You heard what I said,' he grunted, as he got on his knees to retrieve the scattered pieces of charcoal.

A bandaged hand and an upturned barbecue had not got proceedings off to a good start. If Dad was in a good mood he could just about cope with the demands of barbecuing burgers, but woe betide all of us if things went wrong. And things had already gone outstandingly wrong before even one match had been struck!

Eventually the pyramids were rebuilt and Dad gave the coals a good dousing with the 'BBQ Odour-Free Smokeless Lighter Fluid' which had over-wintered in the cupboard under the stairs.

The 'Odour-Free Smokeless' bit was a recent innovation since a barbecue last year when the fumes from the 'Odour-Full and Smoky' fluid that Dad was using at the time had been taken by the wind and blown through an open window into next door's kitchen setting off their smoke alarm and asphyxiating their guinea pig. We don't think that our neighbours, who were out at the time, realized what had caused their smoke alarm to be screaming at their dead guinea pig when they returned but in the circumstances a switch to 'Odour-Free Smokeless' seemed like the best move.

Anyway, the lighter fluid was Dad's insurance against the firelighters not working and the use of both usually meant the coals were glowing at cooking heat in no time at all. He struck the match. He always prided himself with using just one match but this time it fizzled out with a disappointing 'spht'. This did nothing to improve his already frayed temper and muttering something about 'showing the charcoal who was boss' he once again gave it a generous dose of the 'Odour-Free Smokeless'.

Another match, another 'spht'. More lighter fluid, followed by several more matches and 'spht's'! Although the coals were not getting any hotter I could feel the rising tide of frustration raising Dad's temperature more than somewhat. I decided to remind him of some first principles; 'Preparation and *patience*, Dad. That's what it takes to make a perfect barbecue.'

'I can do without your wise-cracks thank you very much. I don't know what's wrong with it. It's never been this difficult to light.'

Just then Mum reappeared at the gate carrying a bag of burgers and buns. "Everything OK? I'm sorry I've taken so long, I expect you're ready for these now.' Her gaze fell on the flame-resistant charcoal and without thinking or stopping to assess Dad's mood she added, 'Oh, you've not even got it alight yet. Are you losing your touch?' She didn't know it of course but it was not the most helpful comment she could have made and sadly for her it set Dad off into one of his moods.

Poor Mum. He almost shouted at her, 'No, I have not lost my touch and I don't need you to come swanning in here making sarcastic comments. If you're so blooming clever you can tell me why this wretched thing won't light. And don't tell me to put any more lighter fluid on the charcoal because I've already drenched it in the stuff,' he added.

Mum looked at the empty bottle of fluid and seemed to be on the verge of speaking. She swallowed a couple of times then said quietly. 'That's not barbecue fluid.'

'Oh and what is it then? Come on then if you're so clever.' Dad was at his worst when he was like this.

'It's distilled water that I keep in the cupboard under the stairs to use in the steam iron. If you remember we finished that bottle of fluid at the end of last year and I washed it out to use for the iron.'

I thought Dad was going to get violent. 'You stupid woman. Why didn't you take the label off? You mean that thanks to your rank inefficiency I've soaked the barbecue with distilled water?'

No answer came. None was required. Anyway he was still going on. 'Well, that's ruined that. I don't know. I come home early for once, I get attacked by carving knives and chased by lunatic dogs and then, as though that weren't enough, this whole venture is sabotaged by my thoughtless wife. I'm going out, he said as he threw his apron on to the lawn, 'You can fix your own tea.'

It was all unnecessary of course. I don't know why he burns on such a short fuse and when he blows his stack like that I don't know how to handle it. Maybe I'll look for some advice.

— • —

Dear David

I know loads of people write to you with their problems so I thought I'd run mine past you.

It's to do with my dad. He s not a bad dad – he doesn't beat me up or anything like that but every so often he just loses his temper over the least little thing. When he gets like that he shouts at everyone in the vicinity, calling them names and blaming them for things that were not even their fault. Sometimes he even storms out of the house and when it's all over he just acts like nothing has happened.

I used to just accept it as 'Dad being Dad' but now it really bugs me and I find that I'm beginning to resent the way he treats us all. I know I should love my dad, and I do – most of the time but quite often these days I find that I'm quite glad when he's not around and that's not right, is it? I want to love him but he's making himself unlovable. What should I do?

I look forward to your reply.

Yours sincerely

Alex

— —

Dear Alex

Families would be great if it weren't for the people in them, wouldn't they? The truth is that, whilst some families certainly work better than others, 'ideal' families only exist in fiction. All families that I've ever come across have good points *and* bad points and each family member has strengths *and* weaknesses. An important part of being a good family member is to learn how to enjoy and appreciate the good points in each other whilst at the same time coping with the bad.

From what you write in your letter there's lots to enjoy about your dad but there's also a lot to cope with! So what can you do? Well, let's be honest. If there was an easy shortcut to changing your dad, you or your mum would probably have found it by now. There's no magic wand to wave over him to make him less moody and there's no 'Instant-Cure-for-Grumps' for you to rush out and buy from the chemists!

God is very realistic about what he expects of us when other people disappoint us. He doesn't expect us to disown them and nor does he expect us to be able to change them. He simply expects us to keep loving them.

You say in your letter that you want to love your dad. That's great because if you'd given up all together that would make the job even harder. There are many reasons why it is hard to love everyone all of the time but before writing your dad off as 'unlovable' let's take a look at what it means to love someone; sometimes we find it hard to know how to love people because we haven't understood what love is! The Bible gives a lengthy definition of love in 1 Corinthians 13. Here is part of it:

'Love is patient and kind; it is not jealous or conceited or proud; love is not ill-mannered or selfish or irritable; love does not keep a record of wrongs; love is not happy with evil, but is happy with the truth. Love never gives up; and its faith, hope and patience never fail.' (1 Corinthians 13:4–7)

Love in the Bible – the sort of love that God expects of us – is not to do with how we feel, but to do with how we decide to behave. I can understand how your dad's moods don't make you *feel* very loving towards him but despite that, you can still *decide* to behave in a loving way. Here are four *loving decisions* that you can take, based on the verses from 1 Corinthians.

1. DECIDE TO BE PATIENT

The word patient (or patience) comes twice in these verses and we're also told that 'love never gives up' so being patient is obviously an important aspect of loving someone. Being patient means giving someone another chance; it means telling them that you care about them even after they've been moody and it means hoping and praying that one day they'll be able to change.

I know that you must want your dad to suddenly snap out of these moods and maybe one day he will be able to, but in the meantime, don't give up on him. Have you ever seen the T-shirt slogan, 'Be Patient. God isn't finished with me yet.'? Well, maybe you should get one for your dad to remind you that God still has some work to do on him!

When he's actually getting all worked up about something there's probably not a lot you can actually do – sometimes you just have to be patient and wait for him to get a grip on things.

2. DECIDE TO BE KIND

Love is kind and it is not irritable – maybe that's two different ways of saying the same thing. If we want to love someone we must decide that, no matter how they behave towards us, we will continue to be kind to them and not allow ourselves to retaliate. Bad behaviour can be catching so watch yourself!

When someone shouts and screams at us there is a great temptation to 'give as good as we get'. If someone puts us down then there is a temptation to 'get even' by spreading some unpleasant stories about them. When your dad gets all moody and upsets you there might well be a temptation for you to 'give him a taste of his own medicine' and upset him with a few sullen moods of your own. Retaliation never works. Oh, sure, it might make you feel better for a while but it only makes things worse in the long run.

The loving way is Jesus' way – continuing to be kind, even when under pressure. Do you know the story in Matthew's gospel about the armed soldiers arresting Jesus in the garden at Gethsemane? Jesus' friend Peter was armed with a sword and when he saw that Jesus was about to be taken away he lashed out and cut off the ear of the High Priest's slave, Malchus. Jesus saw what the hot-headed Peter had done but rather than joining the fight he picked up the ear, caught up with Malchus and miraculously repaired his head by sticking his lopped lobe back in place.

Peter fought wrong with wrong but Jesus gave us the example of combating wrong with kindness – I'm glad that Christians follow Jesus not Peter, aren't you?

My advice would be to be kind to your dad when

he deserves it and be kind to him when he doesn't; I'm sure that way offers more hope for your relationship together.

3. DECIDE TO BE FAITHFUL

To be faithful to someone means to be loyal to them and not to let them down; to stand by them through thick and thin. That's quite easy when the person concerned is being nice to us, but it's a bit harder when they aren't!

Let's get an illustration from Jesus again. After Jesus' arrest he was taken to be interrogated and the methods used were pretty brutal. As Jesus looked up from being beaten and spat at, his eyes met those of his friend Peter, who had followed the arresting party and was now close by, watching what was happening.

Peter was scared that if people knew that he was a friend of Jesus then he would be beaten up in the same way. So when people accused him of being Jesus' friend, Peter bottled out and denied that he even knew him. Now it was at this point that Jesus showed his loyalty and faithfulness to Peter. It would only have taken one word of greeting from Jesus to identify Peter as his friend and thus get Peter arrested too. But Jesus didn't call out 'Hi, Pete'. He just looked at Peter and then looked away again. Even while Peter was betraying Jesus, Jesus refused to betray Peter. He showed his love for Peter by being faithful and loyal.

There may be times when you get tempted to betray your dad – to let everyone know just what he is like at home by telling people at school or at church or telling other members of the family just what goes on. Well, of course, you wouldn't be lying if you told them, but you would not be very faithful or loyal to your dad and you probably wouldn't help the situation much either. (However, I'm not suggesting that you keep it all to yourself because it would probably help you to share it with one or two trusted friends who can support you and pray with you – and who can keep their mouths shut about it!)

4. DECIDE TO FORGET!

Love does not keep a record of wrongs; do you? When someone is trying to change the way they behave one of the worst things that can happen is for old mistakes to be constantly raked up and thrown in their face. I'm sure that you could probably write a book about your dad's failures but that might not be a very helpful thing to do!

A few days after Peter's failure to stand up and be counted as a friend of Jesus, he'd gone back to his fishing business at Galilee. It was early in the morning and from his fishing boat Peter could just about make out a familiar figure standing on the beach. He strained his eyes and recognized that it was Jesus himself standing there!

Too impatient to wait for the boat to row to shore, Peter dived into the water and swam to see Jesus. John has written down a part of the conversation that they had together in chapter 21 of his book. It's very interesting to notice not only what Jesus said to Peter but also what he didn't say!

Remember, Peter had let Jesus down by publically denying that he knew him but Jesus doesn't drag all that out into the open. He could have done, of course. He could have asked what Peter thought he was playing at and 'what sort of friend are you?' He could have accused him of cowardice and betrayal. But (as far as we know) Jesus didn't, perhaps because he knew that it would crush Peter to have all his faults pointed out to him – he already knew that he'd failed Jesus and that was bad enough.

In just the same way, it's quite possible that your dad already feels bad enough about the way his moods and bad tempers keep upsetting family life. If you keep on about it, it's just going to make him feel worse and more stressed and then, in turn, even more likely to get in a mood! A nasty vicious circle. So, try to be like Jesus with Peter; decide to forget and break the vicious circle.

Alex, love your dad. Not because he's always perfect (no Dad is) and not because he always deserves it (because some of the time he doesn't). But love him because God wants you to and because it's about the most positive thing you can do to affect the situation.

Decide to be patient, to act kindly, to be loyal to him and to tear up that record of wrongs. This is no fix-it-quick remedy but in the end I believe that it's the course of action most likely to help the situation improve.

Yours helpfully, hopefully

David

PS You may also find it helpful to read the advice which I give to Darren in the chapter 'Windowkleen and Chips'.

6

How to Avoid Nether Wallop

When there are money problems

'WHERE ARE WE GOING on holiday this year then Dad?' It was an innocent question and I wasn't really prepared for the uneasy look that it brought to Dad's face.

'Er, holiday. Don't know. Haven't given it much thought really.' A pause, then, 'Look, Stacey, the truth is that I doubt we'll be able to afford much of a holiday this year. Money's a bit tight and there are bills that have to be paid before we can think about holidays. Maybe things will pick up a bit later in the year, but I shouldn't hold out any great hopes.'

'What do you mean, Dad? No holiday at all?' I was deeply disappointed. We'd never been rich enough to go abroad but we'd always managed at least a week away in a caravan at Yarmouth.

'Well, you could always go and stay at Nether Wallop with your Gran. She always likes to see you.'

Oh, thanks Dad; thanks so very much. I could just imagine the conversations at school.

'Hey, guess what, we're going surfing in Australia for our holiday this year.'

'Wow, mega. We're going white-water rafting in Borneo. How about you, Stacey?'

'Oh I'm being treated to an all-expenses-paid week in Nether Wallop.'

Have you ever been to Nether Wallop? Probably not. It's noticeably lacking in even the most basic requirements for a decent holiday. No beach, no swimming pool, no amusement arcades, no hot-dog stands. No people (well, none under 65 anyway), no theme park, no Pizza Hut – in fact, no shops of any description. It would be far quicker to say what Nether Wallop has got than to list its shortcomings. It has twelve, mainly thatched, cottages, and er . . . that's about it really.

'Dad, you cannot be serious. Not a week in Nether Wallop!' I protested.

'Well, you could go for a fortnight if a week's not enough,' returned Dad, somewhat missing the point I felt.

'No, Dad, what I meant was that a holiday in Nether Wallop is a contradiction in terms. Holidays are all about fun and excitement; Nether Wallop offers about as much fun and excitement as a bucket of cold custard.' I was impressed by my own argument. Dad wasn't.

'There's no need to get all 'iffy. We can only do what we can do. If the money was there we'd all be off to the South of France like a shot, but as you know, it's not.' His tone told me that the matter was closed, as far as he was concerned.

It always came down to money – or rather the lack of it. Lack of money was why I had to wear my sister's second-hand school uniform, and why when the rest of the class went to France on the exchange trip I stayed in school helping Mr Bateman paint scenery for the school play. Lack of money is why I keep very quiet when my friends are all on about their latest CDs and why I always find an excuse when they ask me to go to see a film with them. Lack of money was about to land me in Nether Wallop unless I negotiated the next few minutes very carefully.

'Dad, are you serious about letting me go to Gran's?' I enquired, deliberately softening my tone of voice.

Dad looked up from his *Evening Post*. 'Letting you go?' he queried. 'You sound like you actually want to go. A minute ago you were sounding off about Nether Wallop like it was a terminal disease.'

'Yes, but that was before . . .' I hesitated just long enough to sow the required seed of doubt in Dad's mind.

'Before what? What are you scheming now?" He was working up a head of steam and I knew just how to keep him on the boil. One word should do it.

'Nothing.' I answered vaguely.

It worked like a treat. 'Oh yes there is. I've known you for too long to know that when you say "nothing" is going on, there's a strong likelihood that "everything" is going on. Now come on, what has suddenly changed Nether Wallop into Britain's number one tourist attraction?' He was really going for it in a big way now. His paper was lying on the table, forgotten, a mark of his concern at this new turn of events. I knew that a few more well-chosen words would do the trick.

I spoke hesitantly, as though I didn't really want to give the information. 'It's just that . . . last time I was there . . . I made . . . a new friend. That's all. It'll be nice to meet up again.'

'New friend? What new friend? I don't remember anything about a new friend.'

'No, well I never mentioned' – (here goes, hit him with *the* key word) 'him.'

'*Him* is it? Boy, then?' he asked, somewhat unnecessarily but it proved that I had him well and truly on my hook. If there is one thing that Dad is more worried about than his lack of money, it's me getting involved with some boy that he doesn't know (he's not too keen on me getting involved with most boys that he does know for that matter!).

'Yes. Terry, his name is. I met him last time I went to Gran's on my own – you know, when you were away on that training course.' Time to reel in the fish, I think. 'He's 21 and he's got the most powerful motorbike I've ever seen.'

That did it. '*Twenty-one! Motorbike!* Do you seriously think that I'm going to let you go swanning off on holiday with a twenty-one-year-old biker. You're off your head, my girl. I'd sooner get a bank loan and take us all bungee-jumping in New Zealand than see you spend a week in Nether Wallop with this Terry and his band of bikers.

What do you take me for? You think you can just do what you want and that I'll take no notice. Well, let me remind you that I make the decisions in this house.'

'Well, most of the time Dad.' I thought.

— —

Dear David

I almost feel a bit guilty writing to you because my problem's fairly small compared to most that you get. I get on well with my parents (well, most of the time anyway) and I've got no real problems at school. So what's my problem? Well, sorry if it sounds a bit selfish, but it's money.

Nearly all the hassles I have are to do with not having enough money. Mum lost her job and Dad had to agree to a pay cut to keep his. I don't think that he was earning much to start with so we've all been struggling ever since.

It's meant things like not being able to go on school trips when everyone else does and having to make do with handed down clothes from my sister. (Things nearly got out of hand regarding our holiday this year but I think I might have fixed that one.) All the time Mum and Dad are saying 'No' to things that we used to take for granted. They make excuses but I know that money is at the bottom of it all.

All my friends just take new clothes and stuff for granted and I feel really awkward being the odd

*one out. As I said, it seems selfish writing like this,
but I'm feeling a bit confused; can you help?*

  Love
  Stacey

— —

Dear Stacey

Thanks for your letter. Don't feel guilty, we all get
hang-ups about money from time to time and I'm
glad that you wrote in because there's nothing
worse than feeling that you are the only one with
your problem and that no one else will understand.

There are, in fact, loads of people in your position. People who find that there isn't enough money
to go around all the things that they *need*, never
mind what they *want*. I'm afraid I can't write to tell
you how to get rich quick but here are a few ideas
that might help you come to terms with your situation, and how to handle what money you have got
wisely.

1. SOME THINGS ARE MORE
IMPORTANT THAN MONEY

Love, for example! It's not unusual to read in the
papers about people who have had everything that
money could buy but still feel unhappy because
they had no one who loved them. It's a fact that
human beings can cope much better with lack of

money than lack of love. We *need* love, but we only *want* the things that money can buy for us.

It seems from what you've written that you get on well with your parents. That's brilliant, Stacey, and I guess that there are many kids at your school who would willingly live without some of the things that they *want* if only they felt that their parents were meeting their *need* to be loved and cared for.

I know that you'd like your parents to be able to give you more 'things' than they can at present. They'd probably like that too. But try to see that as things are they are giving you the best thing that they have, and something that will mean more and more to you – their love.

2. DON'T BELIEVE THE ADVERTS

The world of advertising puts a lot of pressure on us to spend money we haven't got on things we don't need. Adverts are not designed to tell you the truth about the world or yourself. They are only designed to get you to spend your money. They do that by *suggesting* three things

a) If you buy this thing you'll be happier.
b) If you buy this thing you'll be a better person.
c) If you buy this thing you'll be more popular.

Well, it may be true some of the time but all too

often it's not. You know the way it is supposed to work.

The girl in the advert sprays herself with the latest perfume – 'Tunnell' from Chanel. Wearing the Chanel 'Tunnell' she wafts down the staircase in her office smiling contentedly (she's happier).

Men look up from their desks as she floats past them, then look at each other and nod approvingly. Was this really tiny Penelope from the typing pool? (she's become a better person).

Finally she enters her boss's office and although he clearly is in the habit of ignoring his typist, on this occasion he puts down the phone, stands and gawps in wonder at this apparition that's just entered (she's become more popular).

And all because the lady wears Chanel 'Tunnell'!

Now what happens? Thousands of girls rush out to buy Chanel 'Tunnell'. But when *they* wear it either no one at work even notices or someone (who clearly hasn't seen the advert and so doesn't know the correct way to respond) says, 'Cor, what the blooming heck's that niff. Someone trod in something?'

Maybe some of your schoolfriends are taken in by the power of advertising but there's no need for you to be. True happiness is not found by having enough money to buy every new product that comes onto the market. Jesus said that true happiness is found by those whose 'greatest desire is to do what God requires'. He said that God will do something that the advertisers and their products can never do, he will 'satisfy them fully' (Matthew 5:6).

3. BE GRATEFUL FOR WHAT YOU HAVE GOT

I know, I know, you haven't got all that you'd like, but open your eyes, Stacey. You've got so much. It's all a matter of who you compare yourself to.

If you compare yourself to your well-off friends all the time then you'll feel more and more unhappy. But how about taking a look at some of the people in your school who are worse off than you (I'm sure that there are some in worse financial difficulties than yours – you mentioned a holiday but there's loads of kids in the UK for whom a holiday is just a dream).

Or how about looking even further afield to other parts of the world where people of your age have nothing except maybe the few rags that they stand up in. They've never owned a toy, or slept in a house and many times they've gone without food for days on end – maybe they've even lost their parents to war or disease. It's a painful thought, isn't it, but it's reality for millions in our world today and when we measure our lifestyle against theirs we suddenly realize just how rich we really are.

4. BE GENEROUS WITH WHAT YOU HAVE GOT

One of the traps that we can fall into when we haven't got much is that we try to protect it so as not to lose it. When it's taken us a year to save up for our Walkman we tend to be far more protective of it than someone who had theirs given to them and who knows that should they lose it, they'll probably be given another one!

Now at one level it is clearly a good thing to take good care of your possessions – it would be wasteful to treat everything as though it were disposable. But there is a very short step from being careful with what we have to being selfish. God expects us to be careful and to look after things but he does not expect us to be selfish.

In our country we are brought up to believe that we are all individuals and that we must look after ourselves first and foremost. But in the Bible, Jesus taught us that we all belong to one another and that we must put other people first. Jesus taught whole-hearted, open-handed generosity. 'People not things' could have been his motto.

Jesus' first followers took his radical attitude to possessions so seriously that when they started the first church in Jerusalem we read that 'no one said that any of his belongings was his own, but they all shared with one another everything they had.' (Acts 4:32). Now that's generosity!

Even if you still feel you've not got much, start learning good habits and thinking of other people. Share what you have and make God chuffed!

5. THINK OF YOUR PARENTS

If you are finding it difficult to cope with what you have, then I'm sure that it is doubly difficult for your parents. They may not show it to you, but they probably feel terrible about not being able to give you all that they'd like to. From what you say they sound like they may well be going without some things themselves in order that you have as much as possible.

I'm sure that it would really help them if you could let them know that you understand their struggle over money. It would be so helpful to them if you could try to be realistic about what you expect them to be able to provide. Sure, you might want a portable CD for your birthday but is it fair to put that pressure on your parents? You know they can't afford it, yet they may feel that they are letting you down by not being able to provide what you want. So why not ask for things in their price range – they'll feel pleased to be able to get you what you want and you'll at least be fairly sure that you'll get what you ask for.

Anyway, try to keep your sights set on what's really important, Stacey.

Yours helpfully, hopefully

David

7

A Party Popper During the Sermon

When you're not sure about church any more

'IT WAS ONLY A PARTY POPPER for goodness' sake.'

'Yes, but why did you let it off in the middle of the sermon?'

'I've told you hundreds of times. I didn't mean to let it off. I was bored and I found the thing in my pocket and as I was fiddling with the string it just went off . . .'

'Why did you take it to church in the first place? What was it doing in your pocket?'

'It must have been left over from last night's party, I suppose.'

The inquisition went on and on. Dad was in a real strop and there was no hiding place from his fury. How had it happened? My mind drifted back over the evening's events as Dad's disapproving lecture droned on.

It had all started in time-honoured fashion. We'd arrived at church at about 6.15 in time for the 6.30 service. Mr Hewitt was on 'Welcoming' duty and greeted us with hymn books, plastic smile and an eye-wateringly firm handshake. Mum and Dad always sat at the back – right hand side, third and fourth seats in – and as they took their places I went to sit with some of my friends nearer the front.

By 6.25 all the regulars were in their place. Mrs Peters was installed, fully armed with cough sweets which she would unwrap noisily during the opening prayer (no one had ever heard her cough, but everyone had heard her cough sweets). Miss

Milligan, an elderly and partially deaf spinster had taken her usual seat just in front of us (row three, second seat in) and adjusted her hearing aid to take in the pre-service performance of Mr Morgan at the organ.

Everyone was in place as at 6.29 (and 45 seconds) Mr Grimethorpe the minister emerged from the vestry and strode to the front of the church, whilst the short stream of attendant deacons who followed him from the vestry filtered to their places amongst the congregation.

Six-thirty precisely and we were off on the well-known menu of hymns, prayers, collection, notices and Bible readings (one from the Old and one from the New Testament) all topped of with one of Mr Grimethorpe's sermons. The pattern was so predictable that my friends and I had devised a number of mental exercises that could be employed to deaden the dullness of it all. Here's a sample of our 'Lower Loxley Evangelical Church Service Survival Guide'.

1. Count the hairs on the neck of the person sitting in front of you and divide by the number of verses in the first hymn.
2. See how many words you can make out of Grimethorpe.
3. Guess in which of tonight's hymns Mr Morgan will miscalculate and start playing a verse that isn't in the hymn book.

4. Guess how many cough sweets Mrs Peters would unwrap during the service.

5. Pretend that you are a thief and work out the best way of stealing the collection plate without being noticed.

6. Add up all the numbers on the hymn board and divide by the number of legs in church (chair legs, table legs, people's legs could all be counted).

7. Look through the hymn book to find the hymn writer with the most outrageous name (James Augustus Toplady takes some beating!).

8. Guess how many times Miss Milligan would adjust her hearing aid during the service.

9. Work out how many seconds there are between the present time and the end of the service (tricky one this since by the time you've finished the calculation the 'present time' has changed, so you have to start again).

10. Work out what would happen if someone accidentally filled the glass from which Mr Grimethorpe sipped during his sermon with vodka rather than water.

This particular evening I'd worked my way through all ten points of our survival guide and it was still only 7.15. A full quarter of an hour of sermon left and nothing to do but listen to Mr G. in full flow, all about 'the timeless wisdom of God as manifested in the genealogies of Matthew chapter 1'. The only thing that was timeless as far as I was concerned was this service and in desperation I rummaged in my pocket for something to enliven the last 15 minutes of the ritual.

Usually all that my pocket contains is empty sweet wrappers, a bus pass and a foreign coin or two, so imagine my delight when my hand closed on a small plastic bottle-shaped object; a party popper, left over from Fiona's birthday party the previous night. Keeping the popper concealed in my hand I carefully brought it out of my pocket and began twiddling the string round my finger. Here was a new diversion for our list: 'How many times can you twist a party popper string around your little finger?' I'd managed to twist it three times around when disaster struck. With an explosion of flying tissue ribbons, the wretched thing just went off in my hand! The effect on the service was dramatic.

Miss Milligan, whose hearing aid was turned right up so as not to miss a single word from Mr Grimethorpe, leaped a clear 20 centimetres into the air and screamed as though she'd been shot.

Mr Morgan leapt to his feet to see what had happened, and got his foot stuck in the organ pedals, filling the church with a boomingly low-pitched growl.

Mrs Peters swallowed her cough sweet whole and actually started coughing – indeed choking – for the first time in living memory.

My friends, festooned with party popper streamers, literally shook with silent delight at my misfortune and all the while Mr Grimethorpe, who'd turned a sort of yellowish-grey colour, like the true professional that he is, kept right on preaching with barely a pause for breath (although what with the organ booming and Mrs Peters choking no one could hear a word that he was saying!).

The remainder of the service has been erased from my memory banks but here I was now, two hours after the event and still getting a right old ear-wigging from Dad. It wasn't fair. I didn't want to go to church in the first place. I only go because dad and Mum would throw a fit if I said I wanted to go to another church (or, worse still, to no church at all).

I awoke from my reverie to hear Dad saying, '... and if you ever do anything like that again your mother and I will leave you at home on a Sunday evening.'

Mmm, now there's an offer that ought to be looked into. Anyone got any left-over party poppers?

━ ◄ ━

Dear David
I've got a bit of a problem. Any chance that you could help?
    I've been going to church with my mum and dad

ever since I can remember. It started when I was a kid, being sent along to Sunday School and when I was smaller I really used to enjoy it (I even used to look forward to it some weeks!). Trouble is, it's all gone a bit flat and I don't know what to do.

The services are so boring and to be honest I only keep going because I know how upset my parents would be if I stopped. None of my schoolfriends go to church and I'm wondering if the whole thing's worth the effort.

It's causing things to get a bit tense at home and we often get into rows. They accuse me of 'going off the rails' and I'm not really – it's just that I'm fed up with the same old routines Sunday after Sunday.

What can I do? Any bright ideas?

Yours in bored desperation

Tim

—▪—

Dear Tim

Thanks for your letter; it was good to hear from you. Sorry that things are a bit tough for you at the moment. It may help you to know at the outset that your problem is one experienced by hundreds of young people who have gone to church with Mum or Dad as children, and now have to work out for themselves why they are there!

1. THE 'INSIDE' STORY

Church services are about far more than singing, praying, Bible-reading and preaching. You can sit through an hour of all that sort of stuff and feel bored and kind of turned off, or on the other hand, you could sit through exactly the same hour and feel really tuned in and involved. The crucial thing is what's going on *inside you* not what's going on in the service.

Imagine a football match where all the stands are packed with people who are totally uninterested in watching football. You can imagine that the amount of support that they would actually give to the teams on the pitch would be pretty small. If those same people were forced to go week after week some of them would end up feeling like you do in church; wondering 'Why am I here?' and finding things to do to fill the ninety minutes of boredom whilst the match is in progress. The problem isn't with the sport of football or the individual players on the pitch, but with the attitude that the 'supporters' have taken to the ground with them.

In just the same way church services are occasions when God's 'supporters' can get together to praise and worship him and spend time learning about him – but if the people in the 'crowd' aren't too interested in him then the whole thing will seem empty, pointless and boring. On the other hand if people turn up at church really tuned in to God – with a real desire to thank and praise him for all that he has done for them in the past week and hoping to learn something new about him which will help them in the week ahead – then those people are likely to get something out of the service, no matter what happens in it.

You have to face the question honestly, Tim. Why *do* you go to church? Do you go to praise God and learn about following Jesus, or not?

2. NO SECOND-HAND FAITH

I guess that when you first started going to church as a toddler, your parents made the decision to take you because they loved God and they wanted the best for you. *They* decided that you should grow up being taught about Jesus because *they* had decided that he was worth knowing.

However, *you cannot go on living on your parents' faith*. You are now at the stage where you must think about the whole thing for yourself and decide where *you* stand.

The first question that you should address is 'Do I want to be a follower of Jesus Christ (that is a Christian) or not?' When you've got to grips with that, *then* you can think about which church will be best for you to attend. All young people brought up in Christian families have to get to this point of personal decision. It's no longer a question of whether to please Mum or Dad, but a question of whether *you* will be a follower of Jesus or not.

In the Old Testament God's special nation, Israel, had all become slaves of the mighty ruler of Egypt, Pharaoh. God loved them too much to leave them there so he rescued them and, under the leadership of Moses, he guided them through the desert to a special country that he had promised they should live in. Before they entered this land Moses died and Joshua became their leader.

Joshua led them into many great battles against their enemies who had taken over the promised land whilst they had been prisoners in Egypt. After many great victories (and some setbacks due to their sin) most of the land was won back for them to settle in. At the end of his life Joshua assembled all of the people and issued them with this challenge:

'Now then, honour the Lord and serve him sincerely and faithfully. Get rid of the gods which your ancestors used to worship in Egypt and serve only the Lord. If you are not willing to serve him, decide today whom you will serve.'

Joshua's words could have been written down just for you and me! If we are not willing to serve God then we must decide who we will follow. We have a choice. Will we give our lives to follow God? Is he worth it? If not, then we must realize that we are following someone else. Maybe our friends, or our music or sporting heroes. Are you more keen to be like them than like Jesus? Are *they* worth it? Can you really trust your most precious possession – your life – to them? Who are you following and are they to be trusted?

Back to Joshua and the people of Israel. Having heard Joshua's challenge the people stopped and thought about this choice for a moment. They remembered all that God had done for them – rescuing them from Egypt, providing food for them in the desert and winning incredible battles for them in their new land. They reckoned that God was the only one worth giving their lives to and said: 'We would never leave the Lord to serve other gods.'

Smart choice! When we stop and think about it, who is there that is more worth giving our lives to than God? God who created the universe; God who created us; God who loved us so much that he sent his only son to suffer and die as the punishment for our sinful mistakes, so that we could be forgiven. There's a song that says:

I really want to worship you, my Lord
You have won my heart and I am yours
For ever and ever I will praise you.
You are the only one to die for me

No one else could set me free
So I lift my voice to you
In adoration.

That's it. That's what Israel decided. No one else is truly worth it. No one else loves us enough to die for us. No one else who we might want to follow is as powerful as God – or as loving – so it makes sense to choose to follow him!

3. ALL OR NOWT!

But that wasn't the end of the story. Joshua wanted to make one more thing clear to the Israelis. He told them that it would not always be easy to follow God. He said that if they really wanted to follow God, then they must realize that he would not accept half-hearted followers – it was all or nothing. God wasn't half-hearted in his love for them and they could not expect to be half-hearted in their love for him.

God didn't want a couple of hours a week from them, he wanted them to live their whole lives for him. To farm the way that he wanted farming to be done. To make friendships the way that he wanted them made. To do business in the way that he said business should be done. Joshua said in effect, 'Are you ready for the challenge. Do you love God that much?'

Being a Christian isn't just about going to church once a week or about being good when other people are looking. It's about allowing God to direct every minute of our lives. The way you work at school, the way you treat Mum or Dad, the way you spend your pocket money, and the way you treat your friends.

It's perhaps worth noting that even though the Israelis chose to follow God, there were times in their history when they very seriously blew it. They broke their promises and tried to do things their own way, even following the ways of the other neighbouring countries. They caused themselves a lot of pain and suffered great losses because they turned their backs on God. However, God never stopped loving them. When they came to their senses and turned back to him, he was still there waiting for them.

Tim, even if you choose (as I hope you do) to follow God and live life his way, then there may be times when you blow it. When, for example, you swear, lie or fail to handle friendships as God wants you to. When you get it wrong it may be a painful experience for you – and for others who may be involved – but never forget this: God cannot stop loving you. If you will only turn away from following bad advice, say sorry to God and anyone else who you've hurt and turn back to him, he'll always forgive you.

I don't expect that this is the sort of answer that

you were expecting to your question. Maybe you expected me to say more about which church you should go to. But as I've tried to show you, I reckon that your first need is honestly to face the question 'Where am I at in my relationship with God?' Your parents have done a good job in bringing you this far but now you must 'decide whom *you* will serve'.

4. CHOOSING A 'GOOD' CHURCH

Hopefully I've challenged you to consider where you are with God at the moment, but having said all that, it may be that it *is* better for you to look for another church where you can praise God, learn about him and serve him. For some people a clean break with the church where they've grown up can give a chance to work out their own faith without being constantly referred to as someone else's son or daughter!

If you do decide that a move would help you here are eight pointers to guide you:

1. Look for a church where Jesus is talked about a lot.
2. Look for a church where the Bible is used a lot.
3. Look for a church where prayer is taken seriously.

4. Look for a church where they are trying to reach non-Christians.
5. Look for a church where the people really seem to care for one another.
6. Look for a church where there are some other people of your age.
7. Look for a church that is as close as possible to where you live.
8. Look for a church where you can be involved and use the gifts and skills that God has given to you.

Don't compromise on the first five points! There's not much hope for a church where Jesus is ignored, the Bible remains closed, prayer is a low priority and the inward-looking members don't like each other! Be honest about your own church. If it scores highly on the above rating system then don't leave it without a lot of thought and prayer – churches like that can be hard to find!

However, if you do decide a change is necessary, and you manage to find a good church to attend, I'm (fairly) sure that your parents won't mind. Break it to them gently; explain why you want to make a fresh start and the good points about the church that you're wanting to go to, without appearing to rubbish the church that you've been brought up in.

Finally though, remember what I've already said; there is no point changing church if you're not turned on to God inside. It won't make any difference – it's possible to be bored in any church if you don't go there with the right attitude.

Yours helpfully, hopefully
David

8

The Archangel Bill

When your parents are not Christians

H E'D BEEN THERE EVERY DAY for the past week, sitting cross-legged on the pavement outside Woolworth's. The hand-written card on the ground said it all, 'I'm Bill. Hungry and homeless. Please help.'

Surprisingly, and despite his obvious need, he looked raggedly cheerful as he played a selection of Christmas carols on his mouth-organ. Each time someone dropped a coin in his upturned hat, apparently without missing a single note of the carol that he was playing, he uttered a polite 'God bless you, friend.' There was something about him that I just couldn't get out of my mind and as the week went on I thought about him more and more.

How could I help him? After all, it was Christmas, the season of good will, love and peace to all mankind. Bill was a mankind of sorts – and so surely he deserved to enjoy Christmas just as much as the rest of us. I wasn't sure what to do so I prayed about it that night and asked God to show me how to help Bill. I didn't get any particularly clear answers but in my Bible-reading there was a verse that said 'Remember to welcome strangers in your homes. There were some who did that and welcomed angels without knowing it.'

I read and re-read the verse and slowly light began to dawn. So that was it. That's how he managed to stay cheerful despite his awful circumstances. That's how he managed to talk and play the mouth organ at the same time. The answer was suddenly clear. Bill was an angel in disguise. Cool and dudey. A real, live undercover angel outside Woolworth's.

Now what should I do? I'd never come across a plain-clothes angel before. I read the Bible verse one more time looking for inspiration and there it was, as clear as a spot on your nose. I saw what must be done; 'Welcome strangers into your homes' it said and so I decided that I had no alternative but to invite Bill home for Christmas.

I'd made my amazing discovery about Bill's true identity just in time. The next day was Christmas Eve and so it was with a real sense of mission that I got up the next morning and after a hasty breakfast made my way to the shopping centre to meet my angel. As I walked, I rehearsed what I would say. I wasn't too sure how you addressed angels so I practiced a number of alternatives.

'Excuse me, O Winged Wonder . . .' No, that sounded stupid. How about 'Glorious Creature of Light, I wondered if you'd like to come back to my place for something to eat.' Mmm, that was getting closer, but still not quite there.

After pondering a few more alternatives I settled for a plain 'Hi there, your angelship, I'd be dead chuffed if you'd come home with me for a meal and a change of clothes.'

I turned the corner by W H Smith and I could hear the wheezy strains of Bill's harmonica growing louder as I drew nearer to where he was sitting. As he paused to wipe his lips between carols, I summoned up my courage, went up to him and delivered my invitation.

'Hi there, your angelship, I'd be chuffed dead if you'd come home with me for a change and a meal of clothes.'

My nerves had got the better of me but he looked at me, smiled and said 'Well, now, there's an offer. And what would your parents think of a tatty old fellow like myself turning up unannounced on Christmas Eve?'

Good point! In all my excitement about discovering Bill's angelic identity I'd not stopped to think of what Dad and Mum would think. On reflection, I didn't imagine that they'd be too impressed, to be honest, but then again God had told me to help the Archangel Bill and it *was* Christmas. Even though my parents weren't Christians surely they wouldn't begrudge one of God's own messengers a mince pie and a glass of sherry (even Father Christmas used to get that much on Christmas Eve, and Bill was a real live cherub!).

Hastily weighing up Bill's question, I blurted out, 'Oh, they won't mind a bit, they'd be pleased to see you. We often have strangers in our home at Christmas,' (That was nearly true. We often had Aunt Mildred and they don't come much stranger than her!)

Bill asked again. 'Are you sure they won't mind?' I'd never realized just how cautious off-duty angels were.

'Yes, no problem. Come on, it's not far.' A few more moments of reassurance and Bill was shuffling alongside me, homeward bound.

It was only as we walked up the front path that feelings of doubt began to eat at my good intentions, feelings which intensified as we entered the front door and Mum's voice rang out from the kitchen, 'Is that you, Tony? You weren't out long. Did you forget something?'

'Hi, Mum. Could you come out here a minute, I've got a surprise for you,' I called, a seasonal false cheerfulness almost covering my anxiety. Never a truer word was spoken, for as Mum emerged from the kitchen she caught sight of her first-ever angel and, yes, she did seem to get a surprise. Shock might have been a better word for it, because she stood rooted to the spot, mouth frozen in the open position, staring at Bill in what I took to be a most awestruck manner. So complete was her paralysis that it was left to Bill to break the ice.

'Hello, missus. It was very nice of you to invite me home for Christmas. Proper cold it was out there on that street.' He looked around. 'Nice place you got. Reckon I'll be quite comfy here.'

Mum's mouth thawed enough for her to gasp, 'Tony. Can I have a quick word with you in the kitchen? Now, please.'

With the kitchen door pushed to, leaving just enough of a gap for her to keep an eye on our guest,

Mum went on the attack, hissing between closed teeth, 'What in the name of Father Christmas are you playing at? Who is that man and why is he standing in our house? And what's all this about being comfy for Christmas? Answers please, and fast.'

I began to explain about good will and Christian love. About how God had let me know that Bill was an angel in disguise and how the best way to help lost cherubs was to invite them into your home. I even offered to get my Bible and read her the actual verses, but the look in her eyes told me to shelve that plan for the time being! It was useless trying to explain. If only she was a Christian perhaps she'd have understood but as it was she seemed completely closed to seeing Bill as anything but a homeless old scrounger.

We went out to where Bill was still standing. To Mum's credit her voice was calm and disarmingly sweet as she began, 'Look, er . . . Bill, is it? I'm sorry, but there's been a terrible mistake. Tony had no right to invite you back like this. We couldn't possibly take you in over Christmas – we just haven't got the room.'

Bill's face showed no sign of disappointment as he said, 'Oh, I see. Well, don't worry, missus, I thought your lad was probably a bit out of order when he invited me but nothing ventured, nothing gained, eh? No hard feelings.'

He raised a hand to open the front door but

something in his manner had caught Mum off guard. To my surprise and, as she claimed later, against her better judgment, before she knew what she was saying she'd offered Bill a cup of coffee a mince pie and one of Dad's old overcoats which had been put out to be taken to the Oxfam shop!

So maybe it wasn't so bad in the end. The angel was fed and clothed, Aunt Mildred duly arrived (wearing a Chicago Bears American football helmet for some reason) to occupy the spare room unaware that a celestial being had been evicted to make room for her and I'd done my best to do what God wanted done.

It's tough, though, being the only Christian in the house and this isn't the first time that I've had differences of opinion with Mum and Dad over my faith. Maybe I'll try to get a bit of advice on how to handle it before God sends another angel my way.

— ▪ —

Dear David
A friend told me that you were a good guy to write to for some freebie advice. My problem is that I'm a Christian and my parents aren't. They're decent enough and no real hassle (no more than any parents at least) but every so often we hit major grief when God tells me to do something that they don't agree with.

There was a bit of a to-do with an angel last Christmas that I won't bother you with, but more importantly at the moment they keep on at me to give up some of my involvement at church, partly because I can't always get my homework done on time and partly because (they say) I'm getting too religious.

I don't do that much at church. Wednesday evening's worship band practice (I play the drums), Friday evening's youth group, Saturday evening's the Youth Discipleship class and then there's the normal meetings on Sunday morning and Sunday evening. I always get my homework done eventually – even if it is a few days late.

I read in the Bible that we should always obey God and not men (Acts 4:29) so I reckon I should disregard my parents and just get stuck into church, right? Anyway, you're the expert so can you confirm that I'm going about things the right way please (maybe I could show my dad and mum your reply and that'd help get them off my back!).

Yours sincerely
Tony

——

Dear Tony

Thanks for your letter. It was good to hear from someone who is so obviously keen to live and grow as a Christian. You really seem to be stuck into your local church and that's a vital part of living for Jesus. However, I'm afraid that I can't agree with your attitude to your parents. I'm totally sure that

God doesn't want you to live as a Christian rebel in your own home. The Bible has some things to say that might help you so here's a few points to get you thinking.

1. FIRST THINGS FIRST

Paul writing to Christian young people, puts it this way:

'Children, it is your Christian duty to obey your parents, for this is the right thing to do.' (Ephesians 6:1)

You see, as a young person, you obey God by obeying your parents – whether they are Christians or not! God has made them responsible for your life until you are at an age when you must take that responsibility for yourself. If your parents are not Christians themselves there will obviously be times when they don't see eye to eye with you (I don't need to tell *you* that!). Now God's not stupid – he fully understands the tension that's created by that situation. Let's try to look at things from his perspective for a minute.

a) He has placed your parents in authority over you and expects you to obey them.

b) He knows that your parents are not Christians

and that they may not always encourage you to do what he wants.

c) *But* he knows that you *want* to do what he wants.

Now this last point is really vital. God's just as concerned about what's going on inside our minds as in what we actually end up doing. If you are really wanting what God wants, but can't do it at the moment because you are obedient to your parents' wishes, God fully understands. He is more than happy at the moment with your good intentions, knowing that one day you will be old enough to put those good intentions into practice without your parents getting in the way. He can wait.

2. STEP TOO FAR

Having said all that, if your parents were trying to make you do something that was quite wrong – say they were encouraging you to go shoplifting – then the verse that you quoted from Acts would certainly apply. No human beings (parents included) have the right to force other human beings (children included) to break God's law.

In your case, however, it seems to me that your parents are not trying to get you to break one of the Commandments (there's no Commandment that says 'You must attend five church meetings a week'). Rather they are simply saying that at the moment it is not wise for you to spend so much time on church activities when there is homework to be done. (God isn't pleased by your getting into trouble at school, you know!)

When you disagree with what your parents want you to do, it is important for you to try to decide whether you're being asked to take a step too far – to break one of God's rules – or whether it's more a difference of opinion about the best way to do something.

I remember once being approached by a teenager in your position (her parents were not Christians) who wanted to be baptized. Her parents thought being baptized was way over the top but she was convinced that the Bible made baptism a rule for all Christians. What should she do? Was she being forced to break a command of God?

Well, in the end we decided that two seemingly opposite things were true. Firstly, God wanted her to honour and obey her parents and secondly, he did want her to be baptized! How could she do both? We decided together that the best course was for her to tell God that she wanted to be baptized and that one day she would be, but that for the time being she was going to obey him by obeying her parents.

She then told her parents that she still wanted to be baptized and that one day she would be but for now she realized that God wanted her to obey them so she was prepared to wait. Neither she nor I were prepared for what happened next. Her parents were so pleased that she was prepared to put their wishes first that they changed their minds, and allowed her to be baptized straight away!

Not every conflict has such a happy ending (if only it did). I only tell you that story to encourage you to see that with a bit of clear thinking it can be possible to satisfy the demands of God *and* non-Christian parents.

3. DO 'EM GOOD

Peter writes this:

> 'For the sake of the Lord submit to every human authority . . . for God wants you to silence the ignorant talk of foolish people by the good things that you do'

No, I'm not calling your parents ignorant and foolish – but as we've seen they are the 'human authority' to which you should 'submit'! There is an important principle here. You see, if your love for Jesus makes you a real pain at home then your parents will not only moan at *you*, they will probably think pretty badly of God, Jesus, Christians and everything to do with church for apparently making you so difficult to handle. In other words, your grouchiness will give God a bad name! The more difficult you become the more ammunition you'll be handing to your parents to fire back at the church. From your letter I'm pretty sure that you wouldn't want that.

Peter's advice (above) is that you silence their criticism of all things Christian by showing them the good side of Christianity – 'the good things that you do'.

Take Jesus' example and become a servant in your own home. Wash up without being asked, make your bed (more than once a month), offer to wash the car (without charging!); in short, be an example of practical, serving Christian love to your parents. It'll probably blow their minds. They might try to get you to see a doctor! Whatever, it will certainly prove to them that your faith isn't just a selfish thing that takes their son away from them, but something that makes you a better son than they'd ever thought possible.

4. ENLIST PRAYER POWER

Jesus said this:

> 'Love your enemies and pray for those who persecute you so that you may become the sons of your Father in heaven.'

Hopefully you don't see your parents as your

enemies but maybe at times you get close to feeling a bit persecuted (picked on for what you believe). If you do, then how do you respond? Throw a paddy? Lock yourself in the bathroom? Nick the batteries out of the TV remote control? Maybe. But how does Jesus tell us to respond? By loving and praying for those who are giving us hassle.

Prayer releases God's power into our situation. It really does change things. How should we pray for our 'enemies'? How about, ' Dear Lord, Mum and Dad are giving me real grief at the moment. Please get 'em off my back. Amen?' Well, no, that's not really what Jesus had in mind.

Here are four things that you could pray for:

a) Pray that God will put in your mind a clear idea of how to be the best son that you can be for your parents. Read your Bible after this prayer and see if he gives you the answer straight away through what you read.
b) Pray that you have the inner strength to obey your parents and love them – even when they appear to be acting unreasonably.
c) Pray that they'll start thinking seriously about God because what they see in you. If your faith is big enough you could pray that they will become Christians!
d) When they've hurt or upset you or when you've had hassles pray for forgiveness for anything that you might have said in the heat of the

moment which maybe caused them to feel hurt and let down.

These are all prayers that God wants to answer so when you pray really believe that God is hearing and that he will answer!

5. GET SOME ADVICE

It's often hard when you're right in the middle of all the aggro at home to think things out clearly for yourself. It really is worth finding someone a bit older and wiser – and obviously someone who is able to see things from a Christian point of view – to chat it all through with.

So there are five bits of advice for you, based on God's word, the Bible. Write and let me know how you get on.

Yours helpfully, hopefully

David

9

If Only We Had More Aerosols

When parents always seem to say 'No'

M UM WAS IN concerned-parent mode. 'Now look, love, you're sure you'll be all right? It's just tonight and we'll be back by 10 o'clock in the morning. I've left a contact number . . .'

'. . . by the phone, Mum, I know; you've told me enough times!'

Once a year Dad's boss organizes an outing for everyone in the company to go up to London to watch a show and stay overnight in a hotel. This year, for the first time, Mum had asked if I'd sooner stay at home on my own when they go, rather than stay with Aunt Nancy as I'd done in previous years. Although I always enjoyed staying with Aunt Nancy I had decided that being left with the house to myself had certain advantages, so I'd agreed to give it a go and stay home alone.

Today was the day and the nearer we got to the time for their departure, the more stressed-out Mum was getting. She was speaking again, 'There's plenty of food in the fridge. I bought a few extra bits in case you get peckish.'

I'd already been shown the 'few extra bits' and I couldn't resist saying, 'Mum, do you really think that I'll get through half a cold chicken, a tub of coleslaw, four yoghurts, six chocolate biscuits, a pound of cheese, a tin of tuna chunks, half a cucumber, a whole lettuce, two litres of Coke and a bag of oven chips between four o'clock this afternoon and ten o'clock tomorrow morning? It does seem a little over-the-top just for one person for one evening, don't you think?'

Mum was not to be deterred. 'Well, I couldn't bear to think of you starving while we were enjoying ourselves,' she countered.

I was about to ask in which circumstances she could bear to think of me starving but she was off again. 'Don't forget. Keep the door locked at all times, put the cat out at 6 o'clock and don't stay up all night watching the TV.'

This was getting monotonous so I interrupted, 'Really, Mum it's no big deal. You've written all this down and you've said it about a million times. What next, a video version? I'll be OK. Now just you and Dad go off and enjoy yourselves and leave me to pig out.'

It's true that staying in the house alone didn't worry me but I also had other reasons for wanting Dad and Mum to get off out of the way. They didn't know it, but I'd invited a few friends round for the evening and the sooner they went, the sooner I could ring round and say that the coast was clear. Dishonest, maybe, but too good an opportunity to miss and anyway if I asked their permission they'd only say 'No'. 'No' is their favourite word. In fact, they like it so much that they use it all the time. For example:

Me: 'Can I stay out late tonight to . . . ?'

Them: 'No.'

Me: 'Can I borrow five quid to . . . ?'

Them: ' No.'

Me: 'Can I go to Jane's house to watch . . .?'

Them: 'No.'

Me: 'Can I miss youth group on Friday to . . . ?'

Them: 'No.'

I could go on, but you get the drift I'm sure. It doesn't matter what the question or what the reasoning behind it, anything I say in which they even smell a question mark gets the big N.O. so I'd decided not to ask about having my friends round but to just go ahead and organize it. It won't do any damage and anyway, what Mum and Dad don't know about they can't worry about – so it's kinder to them too!

Eventually Mum and Dad were on their way and a few quick phone calls summoned my friends.

Tracey was the first to arrive, followed soon after by Sam, Helen, Angela and Wendy who'd walked round together. The oven chips were just beginning to brown when the doorbell rang. It was Mandy who unexpectedly had brought her new boyfriend Kevin. This was a worrying development and one that I received with mixed emotions. If anything should go wrong and Mum and Dad discover my little plan then the absence of males in the house would have been one of my lines of defence. Kevin's arrival had therefore removed one of the planks of the arguments that I'd been preparing in my head 'just in case'.

Anyway, I didn't have the guts to turn him away

and so in he came. He seemed decent enough, despite his somewhat suspect 'Arsenal for the Cup' T-shirt.

Having eaten chicken salad and chips, chocolate biscuits and Coke we all settled down to watch the video that Angela had brought with her. It was a thriller called *Dye Hard* and was about a mad scientist who'd invented an indelible colourant which he threatened to release into the water supply of Los Angeles unless he was paid a billion dollars by the city authorities.

The film had just started when I remembered that the cat was still in, so I left the room to put him out in the garden. It took longer than expected because he had crept into my wardrobe and I couldn't find him so about five minutes had passed when I returned to pick up the threads of the film. As I made my way back to the sitting room I was beginning to feel quite relaxed. The evening was going well, Kevin had proved no real problem and Mum and Dad would be well on their way to London by now. Great. Back to *Dye Hard*.

As I pushed open the sitting room door I just could not believe what greeted me. The room was filled with a pall of smoke and the smell of burning tobacco hung heavily all around. A quick glance around revealed the culprit. Kevin had lit up a cigarette. He turned as I entered and, all innocence, said 'Hi, Meg. Don't mind if I smoke, do you? The others thought you would but I was sure you wouldn't.' The 'others' – my so-called 'friends' – continued to stare at the TV screen in an attempt to distance themselves from Kevin and his decision to light up.

Calm and reasonable I was not. I almost screamed, 'Put it out, you pin-head. I don't care if you want to kill yourself' (in fact, at that stage I would willingly have helped him to do it!), 'but my parents will kill *me* if they come home and find the house full of cigarette smoke. I don't believe you could do this to me, you stupid, selfish, thoughtless . . .' I ran out of adjectives to describe Kevin, but he had got the message and sheepishly extinguished the offending article. Too late, the damage was done.

Despite watching the rest of *Dye Hard* with the windows wide open, at the end of the evening curtains, carpets and clothing still stank of smoke. As everyone left I wondered what I was going to tell my parents but, still suffering from mild shock at Kevin's sheer stupidity, I could think of no good reason to explain away the lingering smell.

After a poor night's sleep I virtually ran to the sitting room to sniff the air. It was no good, the aroma of Benson and Hedges still filled the room. What was I to do? Calm down, Meg. Think logically. The smell of smoke wouldn't go, so maybe the answer was to fill the house with so many other smells that the smell of smoke was disguised. Brainwave or what? I couldn't get rid of the pong, but maybe I could cover it up. It was worth a try.

I set about the task with vigour. I left toast to burn under the grill while I gathered up every single aerosol that I could find in the house. Fly-killer, deodorant, hair spray and breath freshener – amongst many others – were all squirted in generous quantities over furniture, fixtures and fittings and in the atmosphere of every room. The combination of smells created some very interesting effects and by the time I'd finished the house smelt like a cross between a rose garden, a pine forest, a dentist's surgery and a public toilet. Surely not even Mum's nostrils could discern the smell of smoke underneath all this other stuff.

Mum and Dad returned early. I heard the car pull up at 9.40 and the key turned in the front door at 9.42 precisely. I was in my room as I heard Mum enter the front door. She started to call, 'Meg, we're home. Where are . . . ' A slight pause, then, 'Good grief, what on earth has happened? What *is* that smell? Meg, where are you? Are you OK?'

I appeared at the top of the stairs and met Mum on her way up. 'Meg, what have you been doing? It smells like you've been using every aerosol in the house.' How typical of Mum to be able to analyse things so accurately and quickly, but at least she hadn't noticed the smell of . . .

'And whoever has been smoking? Meg, what *has* been going on here?'

I'll spare you the gruesome details but I expect you can imagine them anyway. Think of the worst strop your parents have ever got into and times it by ten and you'll be near the truth. If only I'd *asked* to have my friends round. If only Kevin didn't exist. If only we had more aerosols! Too late to worry now but maybe I'll check it out before they go away and leave me on my own again.

— —

Dear David
I've heard you don't mind people writing in with their hassles at home, so here I am!

I get on pretty well with my parents most of the time but I get really fed up with them saying 'No' to everything. It doesn't matter what I want to do or where I want to go they always seem to want to stop me. They keep saying 'We only want what's best for you' but how can it be in my best interests to be really fed up all the time?

Last week it happened three times. They wouldn't let me go to the under 18s night at the local nightclub, they wouldn't let me sleep over at a friend's house and they wouldn't let me go to watch Strangler 2 at the cinema (I know it's an '18' but a friend's seen it and she says it's not that bad and I could easily pass for 18).

If I go ahead without their permission I feel guilty and don't really enjoy myself anyway and if I do what they want I feel angry and resentful

towards them. What should I do? All ideas grate-
fully received!
   Yours in a fix
   Meg

— —

Dear Meg

Thanks for your letter. I'm sure you won't be
surprised to read that your problem is one that
nearly all young people wrestle with. Parents *do*
seem to have an unhealthy attraction to the word
'no', particularly when talking to their own children! Let's look at why that is and how you can
come to terms with it.

1. NO IS A POSITIVE WORD!

Have you ever thought about why your parents say
'No' so much? Strange as it may sound, they could
be telling the truth when they say that they want
what is best for you. They may say 'No' so often
just because they love you so much! Let's look at a
Bible verse that defines love:

> 'Love always protects, always trusts, always
> hopes and always perseveres' (1 Corinthians
> 13:7).

Notice the first three words, '*Love always protects.*'

When you love someone you want to protect them, to keep them safe from any kind of harm and it is this aspect of love that often drives parents to say 'No' to so many things that their children want to do.

When children are small they are into all sorts of things and if parents didn't say 'No' when their child was about to use the neighbour's Rottweiller as a trampoline they wouldn't be being very loving (to the child or the Rottweiller!). Here are four main ways that good parents will want to protect their children.

a. Physical Protection

This is perhaps the most obvious. Parents will obviously say 'No' to requests that they believe will put their children in physical danger – and it's quite right that they do so. What would you think of your parents if they encouraged you to walk home alone late at night, or if they suggested that you should accept lifts from complete strangers?

Clearly a good parent will always say 'No' if they believe that their child would be in physical danger if they said 'Yes'.

b. Emotional Protection

You know, Meg, that it's not just our bodies that can get hurt; we can also get hurt inside. When people let us down, poke fun at us or reject us it can be very hurtful. Our emotions can be very powerful and it sometimes takes years to get over the hurt of rejection or mockery.

Often our parents can see what is happening to us before we can ourselves. Say they were aware that a close friend of yours was really just using you and doing you no good at all. In order to protect you from the hurt of that relationship going wrong they might be tempted to say 'No'; 'No' you can't go out with him or 'No' you can't invite her home. They wouldn't say that just to spoil your fun but because they loved you too much to want to see you get emotionally hurt.

A good parent will always say 'No' if they believe that their child would be emotionally hurt if they said 'Yes'.

c. Mental Protection

Our minds are very precious and what we allow into them is very important. If we fill our minds with rubbish we shouldn't be surprised if we start to feel dirty inside. The things we watch on TV, the things we talk about with our friends, the books and magazines that we read, the films we watch and the music that we listen to all help shape the thoughts that go through our minds.

If you ask your parents if you can go to the cinema to watch an 18-rated film (apart from the fact that it would be illegal for you to do so) they wouldn't be very loving if they said 'Yes'. They want to protect your mind from the violence, foul language and sex scenes which may have caused the film to gain its '18' rating. (In just the same way if they felt that a particular friend was having a bad influence on you, then their love for you would lead them to want to protect you from the harmful influence of those 'friends'.)

A good parent will always say 'No' if they believe that their child would be mentally damaged if they said 'Yes'.

d. Spiritual Protection

There is a part of every person which enables us to relate to the unseen spiritual world that surrounds us. The Bible tells us that the world we can see is only half of the picture. There is another equally real but invisible part of God's creation where God himself lives and where spiritual creatures like angels and evil spirits exist. We need to take good care of the spirit inside of us and do all that we can to keep it in tune with God.

There are a number of 'games' and activities such as Ouija, Tarot cards and horoscopes which try to contact these invisible spiritual powers. The trouble is that the powers behind these activities are not God's but those of his enemy, Satan. If you were to take part in this sort of thing then you are quite clearly putting your spiritual health at risk!

The best advice is to leave them alone and a good parent will always say 'No' if they believe that their child would be in spiritual danger if they said 'Yes'.

I hope you can see that 'No' is often a very positive answer from very loving parents. Far from being a negative word, it can be a word which tells you that your parents love you enough to want to protect you physically, emotionally, mentally and spiritually.

However, having said that, two other things need to be said:

2. NEGOTIATE YOUR INDEPENDENCE

Your parents clearly cannot protect you for ever and if you asked them I expect they'd say that they wouldn't want to! But parents are not always very good at taking their hands off and allowing their children to make more decisions for themselves.

It can't happen all at once. When you were first born your parents had to make absolutely every decision for you and as you've grown they have made less and less. One day you will be completely left to make up your own mind about everything but in the meantime you are somewhere in the middle of that process.

Why not try to talk to your parents about where you are on this journey towards independence.

Don't try to talk it through when you are angry with each other or when they've just said 'No' to something! You could ask them for more freedom to make your own decisions in particular areas but be realistic and don't try to get everything you might want at once.

Be willing to compromise as well. For example, if they currently insist that you are in by 10.00 every night and you want to stay out until midnight every night then suggest a halfway house like coming home at 10.00 all week but being able to stay out to 11.00 at weekends as long as they know where you are and how you are getting home.

It should also help you negotiate if you try to find out *why* they are saying 'No' to a particular request. Listen to them and be ready to admit that they might have a point. If you think that their fears are groundless then explain your point of view in a calm way.

3. EARN YOUR INDEPENDENCE

When your parents see you behaving responsibly and making wise decisions about where you go, when you go there and who you go with, they will probably be more inclined to stop saying 'No' to so many things. Their job as parents is to teach you how to manage your own life properly not spend the rest of their lives running yours for you! In the end it all comes down to trust. The more that they feel able to trust you, the more relaxed they will be about leaving you to make your own decisions. On the other hand if you abuse the trust that they put in you (for example, by having friends round when they are away or by sneaking in to see an '18' film) then they may well try to control your life even more. Trust takes quite a time to be earned but can be quickly lost so be patient and be careful not to blow it all in one thoughtless decision!

Anyway, Meg, on balance I think that you should be grateful for having parents who care enough to say 'No' but I also think that you are at an age where they need to begin to trust you to make a few more of your own decisions. I hope that this letter helps you see your situation a bit more clearly.

Yours helpfully, hopefully

David

10

Windowkleen and Chips

When things get physical

'DON'T SHOW IT. Don't show it. Fight back the sobs; time for them later when I'm alone in my room. Why should I give him the pleasure of seeing me cry. Stare him out. Stare him out. Stare . . . ouch. That one really hurt. But don't show it. Not now. Not ever.'

It all started an hour ago. I'd been left in the flat in charge of my little sister. She is only four and a real handful of trouble. Her favourite trick is opening the cupboard under the kitchen sink and making detergent soup out of the various cleaning materials stored there. Half a box of Ultra-Kleen, a dash of Lemon Surface Wipe (why do people wipe the surface of lemons?) and a generous squeeze of Gnome Multi-Purpose Washing-Up Liquid (which not only cleans your dishes, softens your hands and polishes your fingernails, but also dissolves any gold jewellery you might have on your fingers).

Anyway, today Dad had gone out to buy a paper from the local shop and Mum was at work. Dad had issued the usual instructions, firing them in short bursts over his shoulder as he walked out of the door.

'Don't open the doors to anyone – not anyone, mind.'

'Keep your sister away from the fire.'

'Leave the phone if it rings.'

'And Darren, don't touch anything that doesn't belong to you.'

He always said all that stuff, even if it was high summer and the fire wasn't on. Habit, I suppose. Anyway, it was all common sense and I didn't feel too hassled by it – even though I'd sooner not be left in charge of Donna.

Not long after he'd gone out, the phone rang. Leave it, Dad had said and usually that's what I did. However, today it rang on and on and on and before I'd noticed what she was doing Donna had picked it up. I flew across the room and snatched the receiver from her hands just before she could say anything and without thinking, I automatically said "Hello" to whoever was at the other end.

Donna resented losing the chance to talk down the phone and shrieked her disapproval. I couldn't hear what the caller was saying so I took the phone out into the hall and shut her in the sitting room to continue her paddy.

In the quiet of the hall I could hear the voice of my Gran saying 'Is that you, Jenny?' (Gran always thinks that I'm my Mum when I answer the phone.)

'No, Gran, it's Darren.'

'Pardon? You'll have to speak up, this is a terribly bad line. Is that you, Jenny?'

I raised the volume a bit. 'No, Gran, it's Darren.'

'Oh, sorry. I must have the wrong number. I don't know anyone called Karen.'

This time I almost shouted, 'Darren, Gran. It's Darren. Remember me, your grandson?'

Slight pause then, 'Oh Darren, is that you?'

149

Oh grief, this was going to last all day. "Yes, Gran, it's Darren. Did you want Dad? He's gone down the road for his *Sun*.'

"Gone down the road with his son? But . . . you're his son, Darren. It is Darren I'm talking to, isn't it?'

I couldn't go on like this; Dad might come home at any minute and if he found me on the phone he'd throw a fit. A flash of inspiration struck me, I raised the pitch of my voice a bit and bluffed, 'Darren; did you say Darren? No sorry, this is Karen. No one called Darren lives here. Sorry, you must have the wrong number.'

I felt a bit mean putting the phone down on my own Gran but honestly! Gran's got a hearing aid but she refuses to turn it up because she says it wastes electricity. No matter how many times we tell her that it runs off a battery and has no bearing at all on the size of her quarterly electricity bill she won't listen (if you see what I mean).

Peace descended on the flat as I walked into the sitting room to put the phone back in its holder. Hang on a minute! Light dawned slowly but worryingly. Peace was not the normal state of things when Donna was around. I'd forgotten all about her while I was on the phone. Where was she and, more to the point, what was she up to?

A brief tour of the sitting room left me in no doubt that she wasn't there. She couldn't be in the bedrooms or the bathroom because she hadn't gone

past me while I was on the phone. That only left –
oh no – the kitchen.

I was almost too scared to open the kitchen door.
It creaked a warning as I gingerly inched it open. To
be honest, things weren't as bad as I'd feared – they
were much worse.

Donna was washing her clothes. That in itself
wouldn't have been too disastrous except that she
was still wearing them, sitting in the sink scrubbing
her cardigan with a pan scourer in one hand and an
open bottle of Windowkleen in the other.

'Donna! What are you doing? Dad'll kill me. Get
out of there.' I shrieked.

Donna jumped, surprised by my quiet entry and
sudden eruption of anger. It was a pity she jumped
because the bottle of Windowkleen flew from her
hand and landed upside down (of course) in the
vegetable rack. Carrots, potatoes and onions were
all slowly enveloped in pink slimy fluid.

It was at that moment – of course – that I heard
the front door open and Dad's voice calling out.

'Darren, I'm home. Everything OK?'

The feeling of being trapped mingled with rising
fear and prevented me from saying anything. None
of this mess was my fault. I hadn't answered the
phone. It wasn't my fault that Gran refused to use
her hearing aid. My thoughts raced on but they hit
the buffers in a big way when Dad appeared at the
kitchen door. He stood for a moment, speechless,
drinking-in the scene before moving to Donna and

lifting her from the sink and depositing her on the kitchen floor. Then he turned to me and the inevitable questions started.

'For crying out loud, whatever's been going on here? How did your sister get in this mess? Whatever were you doing all the time? You stupid boy, I told you to keep an eye on your sister. Look at her. Just look at her. What were you thinking of?'

'I'm sorry Dad. Honest. The phone rang and . . .'

It was a mistake. Like throwing petrol on a smouldering bonfire.

'The phone? You answered the phone? How many times have I told you? What was the last thing I told you before I went to the shop?'

As he was speaking his eyes took in the pink vegetable rack and his face grew almost grey with sheer naked rage.

'For goodness sake. What's that all over the potatoes? I've never seen such a mess. What is it? I suppose you think we've got money to throw away do you? All that food will have to be chucked in the bin.'

As he spoke he stormed across the room and grabbed me by the arm. He shoved me roughly towards the rack and thrust my face towards it. The pungent smell of Windowkleen filled my nostrils.

'Look at it. It's your fault, all . . . your . . . fault.' His hand tightened on my arm with each word uttered.

He swung me round to face him and I knew what was going to come next. As the blows began to fall I bit the inside of my mouth and told myself, 'Don't show it. Don't show it. Fight back the sobs; time for them later when I'm alone in my room. Why should I give him the pleasure of seeing me cry. Stare him out. Stare him out. Stare . . . ouch. That one really hurt. But don't show it. Not now, Not ever.'

— • —

Dear David

I've never written a letter like this before but I don't know who else to turn to. The problem is that my Dad keeps beating me up. It's not just a good telling off, or even the sort of smack that Mum used to give me as a kid. He really thumps me and it really hurts.

He's not like it all the time but at the least thing he blows his stack and lays into me. Always me — never my little sister. I used to get on with him really well. But since he lost his job and Mum has had to go out to work he's on a permanent short fuse and I live in terror of getting on the wrong side of him.

I've tried telling Mum about it but she doesn't seem to believe me. Even when I show her the bruises she acts as though I'm just making it up to get Dad into trouble. Why would I do that — I love my Dad (you might find that hard to believe, but I do).

Why does he do it? What have I done wrong and

what can I do? I feel like leaving home but I've got
nowhere to go? Please help me.
  Yours sincerely
  Darren

━ ━

Dear Darren
Thanks for your letter. It certainly seems like life is
pretty tough for you at the moment. I'm so glad
that you plucked up the courage to write to me and
ask for help. Here are a few bits of advice which I
hope will help you.

1. YOU MUST TELL SOMEONE

It is really important that you explain what is going
on at home to an adult you can trust. It sounds as
though your Mum is going to find it hard to face up
to the situation. You could try to talk to her again
but is there anyone else? How about a teacher or
youth leader who you find it easy to talk to?

2. IT'S NOT YOUR FAULT

When an adult picks on you and hurts you, it can be
very easy to think that you must have done something wrong. After all, when you were small you
probably did get smacked for being naughty and it's

now hard for you to believe that you are getting hurt for no good reason. However, it is clear from your letter that your Dad's anger is unreasonable. By that I mean that it's not a result of *your* bad behaviour but a result of the way that *he* is feeling. Don't blame yourself. Get help.

3. PRAYER CHANGES THINGS

When we are sad or getting hurt it can be very easy to think that God doesn't care. It is then a short step to thinking that it isn't worth talking to him about the situation because if he doesn't care, he's not going to bother to help. The Bible is quite clear, however, that God is with us all the time – in good times and bad times. The Bible is very honest about the difficulties that we face. Take, for example, Asaph, who wrote Psalm 73 and from whom we can learn the following lessons.

Firstly, it's OK to be honest with God. In Psalm 73 we read that Asaph prays like this: 'Oh God, you have made me suffer all day long; every morning you have punished me.' He was so fed up that he was blaming God (unfairly) for the mess that he was in. Anyway, the point that I want to make is that God doesn't wipe him out for being so honest about his feelings. God loves you, Darren, and he can handle your feelings and your anger. Why not tell God exactly how you're feeling?

Secondly, don't stop talking to God. Asaph (again!) said this: 'I tried to think this problem through, but it was too difficult for me until I went into your temple. Then I understood . . .' (Psalm 73:16). You don't have to go to church to talk things out with God, but *do* keep talking to him and keep listening to what he wants to say – maybe through the words of a friend or something that you read in the Bible. Don't let your confusion about your circumstances put you off keeping in touch with God and your Christian friends.

Thirdly, keep believing that God *can* help you. He's not just a sort of heavenly politician, long on promises but short on action. Listen to old Asaph for one last time: 'When my thoughts were bitter and my feelings were hurt I was as stupid as an animal; I did not understand you. Yet I always stay close to you and you hold me by the hand. My mind and my body may grow weak, but God is my strength; he is all I ever need . . . As for me, how wonderful to be near God, to find protection with the Sovereign Lord . . .'

In other words Asaph had got so uptight about everything that was going on in his life that he couldn't see what on earth God was doing. But when everything in his life had been sorted out a bit he could look back and honestly say that God had held his hand and given him strength to get through the hassles that he faced.

4. YOUR DAD DOESN'T HATE YOU

That might seem almost impossible to believe. When someone hurts us that much we quickly assume that they are doing it because they can't stand us being around. From what you say in your letter that is not the case.

Your dad has had a lot of really difficult things happen in his life recently, and he probably feels really fed up about life and maybe feels a bit of a failure for losing his job (although it may not have been his fault). He is probably worried about the future (for example, how he will pay the bills at home) and maybe he even feels guilty about your mum having to go out to work.

When someone is feeling depressed (really fed up), worried and guilty, they also get angry and sometimes all those feelings come pouring out on to someone else – in this case, unfortunately, it's you!

I'm not trying to make excuses for your dad; what he is doing to you is wrong – and he almost certainly knows that himself. But if you can only try to understand life from his point of view at the moment you will see that *you* are not his problem. He needs help and maybe if you could talk to your mum again, and explain things in that way, she might be able to get through to your dad and help him see it too.

5. TELL SOCIAL SERVICES

If you really have no other adult friend to turn to and things don't get any better, then your local council have specially trained people to listen to your problems. Contacting them might seem like a big thing to do but they are there to help you and to stop you getting even more hurt.

The Social Services Department has to make sure that children in need are properly looked after. Don't worry that they will take you away from home because they have to help families with children in need to bring up children in their own homes wherever possible. ('Children in need' just means a young person who may suffer if they do not get help – and you are in that category.)

However, if they thought that you were in great danger staying where you are, they might think about whether they need to find a place for you to stay away from home while things get sorted out. But they could not just take you away; before they could find you somewhere else they would have to go to court to get permission. If you want to stay at home you have the right to tell Social Services and ask them what else could be done instead.

If you want to get in touch with someone to talk to, you can find the address of your local Social Services in the phone book or in your local library. A social worker will be available to talk with you to see what you want, or they will be able to put you in touch with local voluntary organisations set up to help young people. You do not have to speak to a local authority social worker.

Finally, I really do believe that you must do something to help yourself and to help your dad. Don't just leave it and hope that it'll never happen again because, sadly, it probably will. I hope that this has helped a little bit and given you some ideas for what to do next.

Yours helpfully, hopefully

David

11

Are You Receiving Me?

When communication breaks down

OK SO KICKING DOORS and throwing books about the place might not be the right way to deal with things, but at least it got rid of some of my frustration and anger and it was better than kicking Mum and throwing my little brother about the place! I didn't want to come home like this; in fact, I *didn't* come home like this – it was my welcome home that made me act this way.

For most of the day at school things had gone unexpectedly well. It had been the kind of day that I always imagine happening to other people but never to me. In the first lesson we'd got our maths tests back and I got 17 out of 20. This was the first time I'd got a mark in the teens and it had prompted a break-time celebration in which cans of Coke were shaken and sprayed over all my friends who retaliated in similar fashion with theirs. The celebration had reached its peak when Miss Thorpe entered and caught a jet of celebratory Fanta right between the eyes.

'Whatever . . . Who did that? What's going on in here? Whatever are you doing? Look at this mess,' she spluttered, incoherent and uncomprehending of the great celebration that she'd stumbled into.

'Oh, sorry Miss,' muttered an embarrassed Damon Clark whose Fanta had christened Miss Thorpe. 'But it's a great day, Miss. One the like of which the world has never seen.'

'And I sincerely hope for your sakes that it'll never see such a day again,' she replied, clearly not entering into the spirit of celebration which the occasion demanded. She continued, 'What makes this such a great day that everyone and everything has to be sprayed with carbonated liquid?'

Teachers talk like that. You and I would call them 'fizzy drinks' but teachers have to speak in a kind of code which proves that they've been to university and so 'fizzy drinks' become 'carbonated liquid'.

Different subjects have their own version of this code. For example, in science what any normal person would call a 'rotten stink', your average science teacher calls a 'noxious gas'. In maths a 'squashed box' in everyday English becomes a 'trapezoid' in everyday maths teacher-speak, and in English a 'naff book' becomes a 'linguistically challenged piece of literary art'.

I ask you! It's no wonder we never learn much when our teachers speak a different language most of the time. (Before I leave the subject I should perhaps warn you that this sort of thing is highly contagious. Last week Mrs Brawn, our school cook, had written 'Tarte a la Berger Anglais' on the menu board but when we actually sampled this 'foreign' delicacy, it bore a disappointing likeness to what in previous weeks had been called shepherd's pie!)

Anyway, back to Miss Thorpe and the great maths test celebration. All things considered she was pretty decent about it. She sent us to Dot the caretaker for some cleaning cloths and made us spend the rest of break washing down the desks that had got accidentally sprayed. Under the circumstances we'd got off lightly and rather than feel fed-up at losing break I felt relieved that things hadn't been worse. (If it had been Mr Flint who'd found us we'd have been cleaning the whole school during every break for the rest of term!)

Next lesson was music. Last week Mrs Blare, our music teacher, had warned us that she was going to be away this week but that she was going to leave some work for us to do on the board. Mr Harmworthy arrived to sit with us, carrying a large pile of marking which he obviously wanted to tackle whilst we did the set work.

As we entered the room we noticed that someone had been in the room during break and left several derogatory comments about Mrs Blare chalked in large letters all over the set work on the board. 'Mrs Blare has manky hair' and 'Mrs Blare's a silly mayor' (I think they meant 'mare') and other comments all in similar vein. It was nothing too rude but once Mr Harmworthy had seen it, it clearly had to go. He immediately set to work with the board rubber vigorously erasing the insulting graffiti before he noticed that the smaller, neater writing underneath the insults – which was also being deleted by his efforts – had been our set work for the lesson.

By the time he realized what he'd done it was too

late and the only thing for it was for Mr Harmworthy to allow us to do some 'private study' for the lesson. That was great because it meant that I could do some revision for the science test scheduled for after lunch and finish the maths homework that we'd just been set, thus leaving myself with a free evening.

Lunchtime was OK – hot dogs, chips and doughnuts (very nutritious) – followed by an impromptu game of five-a-side football (Man Utd v 4S). All in all then, it was with an unusual feeling of well-being that I entered room H5 ready for the science test.

Mr Davies gave out the question sheets and we all began, in silence of course, to work our way through the test. It was all about the human body. Most of the questions were quite straightforward and what I didn't know I worked out. For example, there was a question about bones.

Where in the body would you find:

(a) the cranium?

(b) the sternum?

(c) the fibula?

Mmm, tricky. Well, 'cranium' sounds like it might be like the word 'crane' and your arms are sort of your body's cranes – so I guessed that the cranium is an arm bone.

Sternum? Well, the stern is the back of a boat so I suppose the sternum is your backbone.

Now then, 'fibula'. This was more tricky to work

out but a 'fib' was what Mum called a lie and was therefore something you said. Perhaps the 'fibula' was therefore your tongue bone. Well, it was worth a try. At the end of the 45 minutes I thought I'd probably done quite well and handed in my paper with confidence.

The last lesson of the day was football and just to top the day off nicely I managed to score the winning goal in the game. Admittedly it was an own-goal and gave the victory to the other team but it was a very spectacular own-goal. Mr Purdy our PE teacher said it was the best he'd ever seen! The other members of my team weren't so impressed but you can't please everybody all the time, can you?

Now that you know how well my day went you will not be surprised that when I arrived home I was itching to tell someone all about it. Mum was the first 'someone' I encountered in the house and before she could say anything I was off.

'Mum, you'll be pleased to know that I had a brilliant day today.' Mum put down her book and looked slightly taken aback at this most uncustomary of greetings.

Ignoring her air of disbelief I continued all of a rush, stringing the events of the day into one breathless sentence. 'I got a really good mark in maths Miss Thorpe let us off spraying her with Fanta Mr Harmworthy wiped out Mrs Blare so I haven't got any homework, lunch was ace, the science test was a doddle and Mr Purdy said I scored the best goal he's ever seen.'

I paused to draw breath and awaited the tumult of praise that I thought I'd earned by my day's endeavours but Mum's response hardly came up to expectations.

'Slow down. I didn't understand a word of that. What are you in such a state about? And look at the state of your shoes. How do you manage to get them covered in that much mud? I've told you I don't know how many times to take your old trainers to change into if you must play football at break. And what's that all down your shirt? It looks like Coke! That'll never come out. How *did* you manage to get Coke all over you? If you had to do the washing in this house you'd be a sight more careful.'

There was more but I stopped listening. A feeling of intense frustration and injustice welled up within me. I'd done my best. I'd worked hard. I'd got my best-ever maths mark and for once, just for once, almost enjoyed a day at school and all I got was this hassle over a few spots of mud on my shoes and a bit of spilt Coke.

'Forget it, Mum, just forget it,' I shouted as I ran to my bedroom and vented my feelings by kicking the door shut and throwing a pile of books across the floor. I don't know why I bother trying to talk to her anyway. Maybe I'll just keep my mouth shut from now on. That would be preferable to being ignored or shouted down. How *do* you get through to parents?

— —

Dear David
Why is it so hard to get through to people? What I mean is, why is it that often when I want to talk to my parents I just can't say what I want to or else it all comes out wrong and I get misunderstood?

If I'm totally honest I suppose I must admit that sometimes it works the other way round and my parents try to talk to me or tell me something and I don't listen and then all sorts of hassle erupts. And then there are other times when they want me to talk or explain something and the best that I can manage is a grunt or two! (Mum once called me 'monosyllabic'. I thought she was swearing at me but when I looked it up in the dictionary I discovered that maybe she was right. I don't always feel like talking about everything, unlike Mum who doesn't like keeping anything to herself.)

Is there any hope for us? I'd really appreciate some help about how we could improve communications at home so that we can say what we feel without upsetting each other.

Do you understand what I'm asking? Hope you can help.

Yours in a state
Gareth

— —

Dear Gareth

I certainly do understand what you're getting at in your letter. Communication is often one of the biggest problems not only in family life but in other relationships too.

We've all had that feeling of opening our mouth and putting our foot in it, or of saying something in all innocence which gets totally misunderstood. Communication needs working at so here are my Ten Commandments (well, ten suggestions, anyway) for improving your speaking and listening skills.

1. THOU SHALT BE HONEST

Covering up the way you feel or stopping short of saying what you really feel will not help good open communication.

Sometimes it's easier to say 'I don't care' than to admit that we do care and explain why. For example, if Mum's going out for the evening and you'd hoped to spend some time with her she might say, 'I'm going out tonight, You don't mind, do you?'

Now it may be because of the disappointment that you feel inside that you hear yourself saying, 'No, that's fine. I don't care' when really it's not fine and you do care! Of course, it might be difficult to explain and you might think that your mum will think you're being difficult if you say how you really feel but in the end pretence doesn't help a relationship develop to maturity so learn to be honest about your feelings.

2. THOU SHALT CHOOSE THY MOMENT

From your letter I can tell that you have already discovered that there are times for talking, times for listening and times for neither! You don't always feel like answering loads of questions or explaining where you've been and what you've been doing. In just the same way your parents have moments when they've got time and energy to chat in depth and times when they've got other things on their minds.

If you've got some weighty issue to discuss the best time is when your mum or dad can shut out other distractions and concentrate on what you've got to say. They'll find it far easier and you're more likely to get a sensible response to whatever is on your mind. If necessary make a booking, tell them that you'd like to chat something through with them and ask them when they will be free enough to talk. Make a time and date and make sure you keep it free!

3. THOU SHALT KNOW THYSELF!

Another aspect of choosing the right moment is to take a quick spot-check on your own feelings before opening your mouth. If you are really feeling up-tight or angry about something it may be better to wait until you've calmed down a bit before trying to talk it through. Words said in anger are often hurtful and difficult to take back, so before trying to communicate how you feel, take enough deep breaths to dampen down any fires of rage within!

4. THOU SHALT PLAN AHEAD

There is a good way and a bad way to say almost anything. Casual conversation doesn't require much thought since it is difficult to be too controversial when you're saying things like 'Can you pass the tomato sauce?' or 'It's cold today'!

However, when you're sharing more personal concerns and feelings it's more important to choose your words carefully. Here's two different ways of saying the same thing. Which do you think will be more likely to be well received?

'Mum, you're always going out and doing what you want. You just don't care about us stuck at home on our own.'

'Mum, I feel lonely sometimes when you're out in

the evenings. I'd enjoy spending a bit more time with you sometimes.'

The first statement is said in anger (the person has broken my Third Commandment); accuses mum, and probably makes her feel guilty. The second statement is more a request for help and will probably make 'Mum' feel wanted.

It's worth taking time to plan ahead and find the best way to say what you want said.

5. THOU SHALT LEARN TO SHARE YOUR FEELINGS

Communication happens at all sorts of different levels from simple statements of fact ('We had pottery today'), through a more detailed look at life ('We had pottery today and my pot didn't work too well') to the ability to share personal feelings at a deeper level ('We had pottery today and my pot didn't work too well. I really felt upset when everyone laughed at it').

If communication always happens at the shallow level of making simple statements of fact then all those other deeper feelings just get bottled up all the time and that's not good for us. We all need someone (and parents should be included in the list of possible 'someones' here) with whom we can share what's really going on inside – our deepest feelings.

Try to train yourself to be open with at least one person that you can really trust about the way you feel and think. It'll sometimes be hard but in the end it will create a far better relationship with them so it is worth the effort.

6. THOU SHALT CHECK THAT YOU ARE BEING UNDERSTOOD

With all the best efforts in the world people can still misunderstand what we are saying. We might be trying to say that we are really upset about something and are asking for help to cope with it but the other person could be picking up that we are really cross about something and wanting to get at them!

How do we know if we're being understood? Simple. Ask! Just say something like, 'Mum (or Dad), I'm not sure I'm putting this very well. What do you think I'm trying to say?'

It may sound like a dumb question but at least it'll make sure that you are really communicating and not getting crossed wires with the person who is listening. Once you've asked, let them tell you what they think you've been saying and correct them if they've got it wrong.

If more people bothered to check that their message was being received *and understood* then there would be a lot less confusion in the world of personal relationships!

7. THOU SHALT LEARN TO LISTEN

Communication is a two-way thing and all the people involved should feel able to ask questions or put their point of view. When you talk to your parents or friends don't be so full of yourself that they don't get a look in.

Ask them for their opinions and really listen to what they have to say. Give them space and let them ramble on a bit if necessary. They'll probably get to the point eventually!

8. THOU SHALT GUARD YOUR TONGUE

The book of James in the Bible leaves us in no doubt what damage the tongue can do.

> 'The tongue is a world of wrong, occupying its place in our bodies and spreading evil through our entire being . . . Man is able to tame and has tamed all other creatures – wild animals and fish, reptiles and birds. But no one has ever been able to control the tongue. It is evil and uncontrollable, full of deadly poison' (James 3:6-8).

Wow, strong stuff but maybe a good reminder of just what damage our words can do when we speak thoughtlessly. I've already said that it is better not to try to communicate when we are feeling angry or upset and this is the reason why. When our feelings are running high we can so easily be rude or unkind and what started out as an attempt to build a bridge of communication with someone ends up with both people further apart than ever!

9. THOU SHALT – IF NECESSARY – GET GRAPHICAL

Despite all our best intentions and all the advice in the world about 'how to communicate' we can still bottle out of opening our mouth. The right moment never seems to come, or else it comes and we miss it! The right words just don't seem to come and however much we mean to book a date to talk things through it just never seems to happen.

Well, try writing it all down. Sometimes a letter can succeed where a conversation fails. The advantages of a letter are:

a) You can say exactly what you feel without being put off by other people's interruptions.

b) You can think carefully about what you want to say and have several goes at getting it right.

c) You can leave it with the person to read at a time that is most convenient for them.

d) They can read it several times and think carefully about their response before coming back to you.

OK, so writing a letter to your own parents *is* a last resort but it can be helpful and can be a way around those times when something needs to be said but everyone is too scared to say it!

A letter or card is especially nice if you want to say something positive to someone (communication isn't only about problems and hassles!). A card saying 'Thanks for being there' or 'Nice pizza, Mum' would probably mean more to your parents than you could ever imagine.

10. THOU SHALT BE BIG ENOUGH TO TRY AGAIN!

You may follow all nine commandments, add in a few of your own and it may still all go horribly wrong. You may still be misunderstood, ignored, or put down. You may still not explain yourself very well, fail to listen or get in a mood and say something you later regret. Human relationships are like that because they always involve human beings! None of us is perfect but if every time it goes wrong we just give up and don't try again then we end up getting nowhere.

Maybe your parents don't listen. Maybe they've upset you. Maybe they refuse to let you do something you really want to do. Even if all that – and more – is true, don't give up on trying to communicate with them. If you lock yourself into an invisible sulky prison whenever they try to talk to you then things can never improve. Give it another chance – and if it goes wrong again, then give it another another chance!!

I hope you do manage to get the hang of communicating with your parents. I'm sure that as you get older all the effort that you put into it now will be rewarded with a much better relationship with them than you would have had if you'd just not bothered.

Yours helpfully, hopefully
David

12

Sick of Being Thick

When parents put you down

WHY DID IT FEEL LIKE there was a time bomb just waiting to go off in my school bag? Why did I walk home more slowly than usual tonight? I suppose it could have something to do with the fact that I was the unwilling delivery service of my very own end of term school report. Expecting you to carry your own school report home was like asking someone to carry the axe to their own execution – sick. But there it was, that was what I was doing.

I not only walked slowly but also took the long way home; even so I only delayed the inevitable by ten minutes or so.

'Hi, Mum' I called cheerily to the front room where Mum was watching TV. 'I've got my school report here,' I muttered under my breath hoping that she wouldn't hear.

'Is that you, Shelly?' The enquiry came absent-mindedly as the video of last night's *Coronation Street* clearly took priority over my homecoming.

'No, it's Margaret Thatcher. Just called in to see if you had any odd jobs needed doing. You know, washing, ironing, that sort of thing. I'm at a bit of a loose end at present.' The attempt at humour was wasted.

'Don't be silly, Shelly. When I said "Is that you, Shelly?" I obviously didn't mean "Is that you, Shelly?" – who else would come home at five to four in the afternoon? I simply meant "Is that you, Shelly?" – you know.'

Precisely! Ah well, at least this little diversion

meant that she'd not noticed my muttered announcement about the report.

'Got a school report, did you say? Let's have a look at it then.' Foiled again. Dad says that if she'd been around in the Second World War they'd have used Mum's hearing instead of radar to detect incoming bombers. He may be right.

Still hoping to delay the inevitable I called, 'Yes, I'll leave it on the kitchen table. You can have a look at it later.'

'No, wait there, I'm just coming.' Mum's arrival was accompanied by the distant sounds of the *Coronation Street* theme music wafting in from the front room. The video had ended; if only I'd been home ten minutes earlier it'd still have been going strong and I could have made my escape. Life can be very cruel. Mum picked up the brown envelope containing my report with a hopeful 'Now, let's see what we've got here.'

The next few seconds seemed like several hours. Mum's scrutiny of my report was punctuated by the occasional, 'Oh, Shelly' and 'Really, love'. Eventually this verbal version of the Chinese water torture came to an end and Mum looked at me with the mixture of pity, anxiety and frustration that she usually gave to our dog when he'd been sick on the carpet.

I could bear it no longer. 'Well. How did I do? Don't just stand there looking at me like that. Speak.'

Mum almost groaned, 'I don't know where to start.' She scanned the report again. Choosing a comment apparently at random she read "Shelly's insistence on using a foreign language in class is most disruptive." '

'Mum, what am I supposed to do in French? We all have to speak in French, all the time. Even Mr James does. What's he on about?' It seemed unfair; grossly unfair. I was about to continue to argue my case when Mum added, 'That comment was written by your maths teacher, Shelly.'

'Oh.' Well, it was a stupid subject and as far as I was concerned Maths *was* a foreign language. So I'd decided to make the point by speaking in Manganese (a language that I'd made up especially for the occasion).

Mum was reading again. 'Since Shelly broke her glasses she has struggled to see the board or read from her books and is consequently well behind with her classwork this term.' Mum looked at me, perplexed. 'But Shelly, you don't wear glasses. You've never worn glasses. What is Miss . . .' she referred to the report, 'Miss Hardiman talking about. Has she got the wrong pupil?'

If only she had. Pretending that you had lost or broken glasses that you had never even owned was the oldest labour-saving trick in the book. Surely Mum knew how pointless humanities was. I mean, what is the point in learning how the ancient Incas milked their llamas? I suppose that if one day you were out for an afternoon stroll in the High Andes (happens all the time) you might be likely to come across an ancient Inca-person desperately struggling to survive for the lack of the skill. You could step right in and say, 'Hey there, Mr Inca, don't you even know how to milk your own llama? Goodness me, even I know that, thanks to my humanities teacher Miss Hardiman. Whoever did you have for humanities? I bet you had Mr Ford, didn't you. He only teaches useless things like . . .'

'Shelly, are you listening? I'm talking to you.' Mum's rising anger cut across my daydream. 'What does this mean? There had better be a pretty good explanation, my girl'.

That was it. Bad sign. When Mum called me her 'girl' I knew that I was in for it. She continued. 'From Mr Taylor, your art teacher: "Shelly's insistence on wearing a diving mask and snorkel in class has seriously impaired her ability to create anything of note this term." A *snorkel*? In *art*? Shelly, what's going on?'

'Mum, it stinks in that art room. It's right next to the kitchens and you get this awful whiff of boiling cabbage and frying fish. I was just making a point, that's all. It can't be healthy to have to sit in that environment . . .'

'No, and it's not going to be very healthy in your environment here when I've finished with you. I'm really disappointed. You're a lazy, good-for-nothing. You're even thicker than your brother and

183

that takes some doing. Why do you do it? You know you'll only get yourself in trouble. You've always been difficult, right from birth but this just about tops the lot. Don't know why we ever bothered to have you – course we didn't mean to, but that's another story. Your sister always did so well. Why couldn't you be more like her?'

On and on and on and on. Go on Mum, tell me again, in case I didn't catch it last time or the time before or the time before that. Thick, am I? Stupid? Unwanted? Careless? I know, I know, I've heard it all before.

— • —

Dear David

I hope you don't mind me writing to you but I really need someone to turn to. I don't know where to start but there's no one around here who understands so I thought I'd give you a go (sorry if that sounds like you're the last resort – but maybe you are).

A lot of the time I just wish that I'd never been born. I've got few friends and Mum and Dad both hate me. They're always telling me how stupid I am and how I let them down all the time. Dad's always at work and most of the time I honestly think that he manages to forget that I exist. Mum's too interested in herself, TV and my sister Angela (in that order) to pay any attention to me.

School's going from bad to worse. The teachers

all think I'm a lost cause as well. OK, I do muck about a bit, and my mates used to think that I was a good laugh but now they're fed up with me and just call me names all the time. Even my church youth group leader would prefer to spend time with the kids who've got brains.

I'm so useless and so fed up, I don't know what to do. Sometimes I think that everyone would be happier if I just ceased to exist; maybe they are right. Mum's always reminding me that I should never have been born anyway.

Please help me
Shelly

—•—

Dear Shelly
Hang on in there. Don't give up. I know exactly how you feel and believe me, you are definitely not (repeat *not*) a lost cause. It's clear to me that you've had a lot of knocks and put-downs which have really hurt you and when we get hurt we don't always see things very clearly so let's try to take a fresh look at a few of the issues involved.

1. EVERYONE IS SPECIAL

That includes you! Who says so? Not your parents, maybe; not your friends or teachers by the sound of it; but this opinion of you comes from someone who *never* lies and who *never* makes a mistake. His name? God.

Did you realize that you are the best thing that God ever thought of? Well, OK, not just you but you and all human beings. It's right there in Genesis chapter 1. As each new bit of the world came into being, God stepped back and took a look to see how things were shaping up. As light first appeared, we read that he was 'pleased with what he saw (Genesis 1:4). He felt the same after looking at the land, sea, plants, sun, moon, stars and all animal life; each time we are told that he 'was pleased with what he saw (Genesis 1: 10, 12, 17, 21, 25).

Finally God made humanity, the most special part of all that he had made because *only* human beings were to resemble him. Everything else had been made *by* him, but humans were made *by* him and *like* him. Not surprising then that when he stepped back and looked at the world now, he wasn't simply 'pleased', he was '*very* pleased' (Genesis 1: 31).

Humans were (and are) simply the best part of the world and Shelly, this might shock you, but *you* are one of those humans of whom God thinks so highly. OK, your parents may not have planned to have you but the moment that you were conceived God was thrilled at the prospect of another human being coming into his world. There's a lovely verse in Psalm 139 which says,

'You created every part of me;
You put me together in my mother's womb.
When my bones were being formed,
Carefully put together in my mother's womb,
When I was growing there in secret,
You knew that I was there –
You saw me before I was born.'

There you go. Not an accident but a special unique person put together by God himself. What more do you want? When you were born he was delighted and, do you know what?, he still is today. No matter what you've done since birth, or what other people have done to you or said to you, God is still totally sold out on you.

2. NO SUCH THING AS A USELESS LIFE

God didn't go to all that trouble to bring you into the world only to leave you on the scrapheap. God can take everything you are and everything that you've experienced in life – the good things and the bad – and make something special out of them. The Bible says that 'we know that in all things God works for good with those who love him' (Romans 8:28).

Some of the people in the Bible had the most difficult upbringings imaginable but God was still able to give them a place in his plans. Moses, for example, was born as a refugee in a foreign country and nearly killed as a baby by King Pharaoh. His mum had to keep him hidden away for three months and then, in despair, she hid him in a basket, floating at the edge of the River Nile – hardly your average childhood, is it? Although saved from the Nile by Pharaoh's daughter Moses really blew it when, as a young man, he murdered someone and had to run away to the country of Midian to escape execution. What a mess! Refugee, abandoned, unsure of his own identity, a murderer. If ever a man should have had a chip on his shoulder, perhaps it should have been Moses.

But this was the very same man whom God chose to play the major part in Israel's dramatic escape from Egypt. The same man who God directed to perform miracles in the desert and who was thought fit to receive the Ten Commandments from God.

Shelly, if God could turn Moses' life around, I'm sure that he can do the same for you. Don't give up on yourself because God has a use for your life. It may not be clear at the moment what that is, but there is no life that God cannot use – he is the ultimate recycler of lives that other people have thrown in the dustbin.

3. WORDS ARE DANGEROUS

It seems clear from what you have written to me that you have been really hurt by things that have been said to you. Do you know the old saying 'Sticks and stones can break my bones but words can never hurt me'? It's a load of old tosh, isn't it? Everyone knows that words *do* hurt us, sometimes very deeply.

The Bible's a bit more realistic. Here's what Proverbs 12:18 say:

'Thoughtless words can wound as deeply as any sword.'

And the damage is even greater when the words come from people who we love and who we want to love us – people like parents, for example!

When we get hurt by other people's words we can react in a number of different ways.

a. Believe

We can believe and live up to (or down to!) their expectations. So if we're called 'thick' enough, we'll start not trying too hard at school – almost as though we want to prove them right!

b. Retreat

We can try and back away from the people who are hurting us. Shutting ourselves away in our bedrooms, spending long hours round at friends' houses or just ignoring our parents even when we are with them are all ways of trying, tortoise-like, to retreat into our protective shell.

c. Retaliate

When we get hurt enough we may feel that the only option we've got left is to fight back. There are several ways that people do this (none of them in the end at all helpful!). Some people try to hurt their parents by being rude to or about them, others deliberately fail at school because they know that their parents will be upset. In extreme cases, when young people have been really hurt they might even try to damage themselves – maybe by refusing to eat normally – just to get their own back on their parents.

You see how powerful words can be, and how much damage they can cause. They are like little sparks that light a great bonfire of hurt and resentment which, once it's ablaze inside us can get out of control, damaging not only ourselves but others around us too.

This is all a bit depressing! So what can be done? Well, negative words are at their most dangerous when we start believing them. As long as we can ignore them or laugh them off it's not so bad but once they lodge in our minds we're in trouble. We need an antidote – something that helps us deflect the lies, so make sure you have a healthy diet of *truth* to take away the bad taste of the lies.

4. Eat Truth

As we've seen, the hurt which you have experienced has been largely brought about because other people have consistently put you down. What's made it worse is that you have begun to believe their lies. Just look at your own letter; do you really believe that you're 'useless' and wish that you'd 'never been born'?

The best medicine that I know of for someone that has been hurt by lies is to eat a regular diet of truth! Earlier in my letter I explained that you are special – that your life has a value not because of what you can do but because of who you are. What's more, your life is useful – God has a plan for your life, something that you and only you can do.

Some people find it helpful to write out some of these statements of truth on pieces of card as reminders of God's perspective on their life. You could carry one in your schoolbag and sneak a look if things get tough at school or pin one up in your bedroom so that at the beginning and end of the day, whatever people have said, you can remind yourself of the truth.

You could start by copying this Bible bit out. It's from Isaiah chapter 42.

'Do not be afraid – I will save you.
I have called you by name – you are mine.
When you pass through deep waters I will be with
　　you.
When you pass through fire, you will not be burnt;
The hard trial that comes will not hurt you.
For I am the Lord your God, The holy God of Israel
　　who saves you.
. . . You are precious to me and . . . I love you and
　　give you honour. Do not be afraid – I am with
　　you'

(These promises were first written to Israel but are true for anyone who loves God.)

Finally, just one bit of practical advice. Try to find at least one good friend whom you can trust and who doesn't join in when other people begin to put you down. If there is even one person in your life who is saying something positive to you and about you then you'll find it much easier to swallow these 'truth tablets'!

5. Healed People Don't Need Bandages

As you have admitted in you letter, you've started to muck about at school, presumably so that people will pay you a bit of attention. Because you've felt unwanted and because you've begun to believe the negative things that people have said about you, you've started to act out of character – doing things that aren't really you at all just to get noticed.

You haven't told me, but it may be the same at home, doing or saying things that aren't really you; things that are just covering up how you really feel. Behaving stupidly or even unkindly can be just an act that you put on to try to cover up the hurts. The trouble is that if you're not careful the stupidity becomes a habit and you can't stop even when you want to.

Don't get started on that slippery slope, Shelly, it's never worth it. If you let other people's hurt change you into an unpleasant person then they've won, haven't they?

People will find you far easier to like and respect you if you act like the real Shelly. I know it seems risky to you and you've been hurt that way before but it's a risk that you'll have to face one day. You can't go all through your life trying to be someone else in order to cover up your hurts. Be yourself and you'll probably find that people will start accepting you far more than when you're being someone else!

It would be nice if everyone else would start

being nice to you first but that's probably not going to happen. If your parents and maybe some of your schoolfriends see you trying to be different that may well encourage them to treat you differently.

How about taking time to talk with your mum and dad rather than ignoring them and shutting yourself in your room? Even if at first they don't respond, keep trying. How about trying a bit harder at school? Remember it's you that'll lose out in the end, not your teachers or your friends, so why go on hurting yourself?

Anyway, I hope that somewhere in all this advice you can find something that helps you begin to value yourself in the way that God values you and that sooner rather than later you eat enough truth to begin to realize just what a special a person you really are.

Yours helpfully, hopefully
David